John Hely-Hutchinson

The Commercial Restraints of Ireland

considered in a series of letters to a noble lord - Containing an historical account of

the affairs of that kingdom

John Hely-Hutchinson

The Commercial Restraints of Ireland
*considered in a series of letters to a noble lord - Containing an historical account of the affairs
of that kingdom*

ISBN/EAN: 9783337238506

Printed in Europe, USA, Canada, Australia, Japan

Cover: Foto ©Andreas Hilbeck / pixelio.de

More available books at **www.hansebooks.com**

THE

COMMERCIAL RESTRAINTS

OF

RELAND

CONSIDERED.

THE
COMMERCIAL RESTRAINTS
OF
IRELAND
CONSIDERED.
IN A
SERIES OF LETTERS
TO A
NOBLE LORD.
CONTAINING
AN HISTORICAL ACCOUNT
OF THE
AFFAIRS OF THAT KINGDOM,
SO FAR AS THEY RELATE TO THIS SUBJECT.

———*I will awake a higher senfe,*
A love that grafps the happinefs of millions.

THOMPSON.

D U B L I N:

PRINTED BY WILLIAM HALLHEAD, No. 63, DAME-STREET.

M.DCC.LXXIX.

To the R E A D E R.

T H E numerous references in thofe letters will, it is hoped, be excufed, when the motive for giving the reader that trouble is confidered. In a fubject of great importance an anonymous writer thought he fhould take too much liberty, in mentioning facts or opinions from himfelf.

He

He has therefore reforted to the ftatute books and journals of parliament in both kingdoms, and to fome
of the moft approved commercial
authorities among the Englifh writers. The hiftory of thofe proceedings feems not to be fufficiently
underftood in either kingdom ; an
attempt to collect it from the many
journals and acts of parliament, in
which it lies difperfed, may poffibly
affift thofe who enquire after truth,
and wifh to form fair and candid
conclufions for the good of the
whole Britifh Empire. In the confideration of this fubject it was neceffary

ceſſary to depart from the chrono-
logical order. The great and frequent diſtreſſes of Ireland during
this century are particularly ſtated,
and carefully examined, through the
many different ſtages of her real
poverty and imaginary wealth. From
thoſe diſtreſſes, as through uniform
effects, the cauſes are traced. The
diſcouragement of the woollen manufactures, by the Engliſh act of
1699, as the principal cauſe, is then
conſidered ; the objections ariſing
from the difference of taxes in the
two kingdoms removed ; and the
advantages that muſt ariſe to Great
Britain

Britain by the repeal of this law ftated. It is then fhewn that no equivalent was given to Ireland for the lofs of the woollen trade ; that the encouragement of the linen manufacture was not an equivalent at the time, and if it was, has long ceafed to be fo. The principle of the act of 1699 is proved not to be juftly applicable to Ireland, confi-dered with a view to the natural productions, or to the ancient com-mercial fyftem of that kingdom; the many Englifh and Irifh ftatutes which eftablifhed that fyftem are ftated down to the year 1663, when

the

the commercial reftraints firft began. Thofe which arife from the
plantation laws, and which began
in that year, are then confidered,
and their effects fhewn on the manufacture, commerce, and navigation
of Ireland. This fyftem of reftraints, if it can be fuppofed to
have been reafonable at the time
when it was introduced, is proved to
be now ruinous to Ireland and to the
Britifh empire.

The advantages over Ireland,
which Great Britain poffeffes in every branch of trade and manufacture,

are

are confidered in the laft place ; and it is fhewn that if the act of 1699 was repealed, fhe would ftill retain a great fuperiority in the woollen trade. Several of the many other reftrictions, under which Ireland labours, are alfo mentioned.

The difcouragement of the woollen manufactures, and the plantation reftraints, are principally infifted upon, becaufe they are thought to be the principal caufe of its weaknefs and poverty; but it is not prefumed to draw any line on a fubject under the confideration of the legi-

flatures

flatures of both kingdoms. Facts
are stated, confequences deduced,
obfervations made, and the principal
grievances are pointed out, the
remedies are fubmitted to thofe who
have the power to redrefs.

CON-

T H E

C O N T E N T S.

FIRST LETTER.

THE diftrefs of Ireland proved to be great and general.————The tempo-rary caufes of this diftrefs.————There muft be fome permanant caufe, and why					1

SE -

SECOND LETTER.

This permanent caufe traced from its effects, by confidering the ftate of Ireland at different periods.——From the
fettlement of Ireland by James, to the
year 1641.——From the reftoration to
the year 1688.——From thence to the
year 1699, when the act was paffed in
England reftraining the exportation of
all woollen manufactures from Ireland.——In former periods that country advancing in wealth and improvements. ——Its poverty and diftrefs from
1699 to the end of Queen Ann's
reign.——The woollen manufactures the
fource of induftry in Ireland in 1699,
and the difcouragement of them the
principal caufe of this diftrefs.——The
fame caufe continues to operate, and
has ftequently reduced Ireland to great
mifery, notwithftanding the encouragement

T H I R D   L E T T E R.

F O U R T H   L E T T E R.

F I F T H   L E T T E R.

b   prejudice

SIXTH LETTER.

The woollen the principal trade of Ireland in 1699.———The linen not then an equivalent, nor accepted as fuch. ———The

S E V E N T H   L E T T E R.

EIGHTH LETTER.

The ftate of Ireland at the time of making thofe laws totally different from the
prefent.

N I N T H   L E T T E R.

T H E

THE

COMMERCIAL RESTRAINTS

OF

IRELAND

CONSIDERED.

FIRST LETTER.

B

T H E

COMMERCIAL RESTRAINTS

O F

I R E L A N D

C O N S I D E R E D.

FIRST LETTER.

My Lord,

Dublin, 20th Aug. 1779.

YOU defire my thoughts on the affairs
of Ireland; a fubject little confidered, and
confequently not underflood in England.
The Lords and Commons of Great Britain
have addreffed his Majefty to take the diftreffed and impoverifhed ftate of this country
into confideration ; have called for information, and refolved to purfue effectual
methods for promoting the common ftrength,
wealth and commerce of both kingdoms;
and his Majefty has been pleafed to exprefs,
in his fpeech from the throne, his entire ap-

B 2   probation

probation of their attention to the prefent
ftate of Ireland.

The occafion calls for the affiftance of
every friend to the Britifh empire: thofe
who can give material information are
bound to communicate it. The attempt
however is full of difficulty; it will require
more than ordinary caution to write with
fuch moderation as not to offend the prejudices of one country, and with fuch
freedom as not to wound the feelings of the
other.

The prefent ftate of Ireland teems with
every circumftance of national poverty.
Whatever the land produces is greatly reduced in its value : wool is fallen one half
in its ufual price ; wheat one third ; black
cattle of all kinds in the fame proportion,
and hides in a much greater: buyers are
not had without difficulty at thofe low rates,
and from the principal fairs men commonly
return with the commodities they brought
there: rents are every where reduced, in
many places it is impoffible to collect them:
                                                    the

the farmers are all diſtreſſed, and many of them have failed : when leaſes expire, tc-nants are not eaſily found: the landlord is often obliged to take his lands into his own hands, for want of bidders at reaſon-able rents, and finds his eſtate fallen one fourth in its value. The merchant juſtly complains that all buſineſs is at a ſtand, that he cannot diſcount his bills, and that neither money nor paper circulates. In this and the laſt year, above twenty thouſand manufacturers, in this metropolis, were re-duced to beggary for want of employment ; they were for a conſiderable length of time ſupported by alms ; a part of the contri-bution came from England, and this aſſiſ-tance was much wanting from the general diſtreſs of all ranks of people in this country. Public and private credit are an-nihilated : parliament, that always raiſes money in Ireland on eaſy terms, when there is any to be borrowed in the country, in 1778 gave 7½l. per cent. in annuities, which in 1773 and 1775 were earneſtly ſou ... af-ter at 6l. then thought to be a very high te. The expences of a country, nearly bankru t, muſt

muſt be inconſiderable ; almoſt every
branch of the revenue has fallen ; and the
receipts in the treaſury for the two years,
ending lady-day, 1779, were lcfs than thoſe
for the two years, ending lady-day, 1777,
deducting the ſums received on account of
loans in each period, in a ſum of 334,900l.
18s. 9½d. : there was due on the 25th of
March laſt, on the eſtabliſhments, and for
extraordinary expences, an arrear amounting to 373,706l. 13s. 6½d. : a ſum of
600,000l. will probably be now wanting
to ſupply the deficiencies on the eſtabliſhments and extraordinary charges of government : and an annual ſum of between
50 and 60,000l. yearly, to pay intereſt and
annuities : in the laſt ſeſſion 466,000l.
was borrowed ; if the ſum wanting could
now be raiſed, the debt would be increaſed
in a ſum of above 1,000,000l. in lefs than
three years, and if the expences and the revenues ſhould continue the ſame as in the
laſt two years, there is a probability of
an annual deficiency of 300,000l. The
nation in the laſt two years has not been
able to pay for its own defence; a militia
law,

law, paffed in the laft feffion, could not be carried into execution for want of money. Inftead of paying forces abroad *, Ireland has not been able in this year to pay the forces kept in the kingdom: it has again relapfed into its ancient ftate of imbecility, and Great Britain has been lately obliged to fend over money to pay the army † which defends this impoverifhed country.

Our diftrefs and poverty are of the utmoft notoriety; the proof does not depend folely upon calculation or eftimate, it is palpable in every public and private tranfaction, and is deeply felt among all orders of our people.

This kingdom has been long declining. The annual deficiency of its revenues for the payment of the public expences, has been, for many years, fupplied by borrowing.

---

* On account of the inability of Ireland, Great Britain fince Chriftmas, 1778, relieved her from the burden of paying forces abroad.

† A fum of 50,000l. has been lately fent from England for that purpofe.

ing. The American rebellion, which confiderably diminifhed the demand for our linens ;
an embargo on provifions continued for three
years *, and highly injurious to our victualling
trade ; the increafing drain of remittances to
England for rents, falaries, profits of offices,
penfions and intereft, and for the payment
of forces abroad, have made the decline
more rapid, but have not occafioned it.

If we are determined to inveftigate the
truth, we muft affign a more radical caufe :
when the human or political body is unfound
or infirm, it is in vain to inquire what accidental circumftances appear to have occafioned thofe maladies which arife from the
conftitution itfelf.

If

* By a Proclamation, dated the 3d of February, 1776,
on all fhips and veffels, laden in any of the ports in this
kingdom, with provifions of any kind, but not to extend
to fhips carrying falted beef, pork, butter and bacon into
Great Britain, or provifions to any part of the Britifh
empire, except the Colonies mentioned in the faid proclamation. 4th of January, 1779, taken off as far as it
relates to fhips carrying provifions to any of the ports of
Europe.

If in a period of fourfcore years of pro-
found internal peace, any country fhall appear to have often experienced the extremes
of poverty and diftrefs; if at the times of
her greateft fuppofed affluence and profperity, the flighteft caufes have been fufficient
to obftruct her progrefs, to annihilate her
credit, and to fpread dejection and difmay
among all ranks of her people ; and if fuch
a country is bleffed with a temperate climate
and fruitful foil, abounds with excellent harbours and great rivers, with the neceffaries
of life and materials of manufacture, and is
inhabited by a race of men, brave, active and
intelligent, fome permanent caufe of fuch
difaftrous effects muft be fought for.

If your veffel is frequently in danger of
foundering in the midft of a calm ; if by
the fmalleft addition of fail fhe is near over-
fetting, let the gale be ever fo fteady, you
would neither reproach the crew, nor ac-
cufe the pilot or the mafter ; you would
look to the conftruction of the veffel, and
fee how fhe had been originally framed,
and whether any new works had been
added

added to her, that retard or endanger her courſe.

But for ſuch an examination more time and attention are neceſſary than have been uſually beſtowed upon this ſubjeᦰ in Great Britain; and as I have now the honour to addreſs a perſon of rank and ſtation in that kingdom on the affairs of Ireland, I ſhould be brief in my firſt audience, or I may happen never to obtain the favour of a ſecond.

I have the honour to be, my lord, &c.

.

THE

THE

COMMERCIAL RESTRAINTS

OF

IRELAND

CONSIDERED.

SECOND LETTER.

THE

COMMERCIAL RESTRAINTS

OF

IRELAND

CONSIDERED.

SECOND LETTER.

MY LORD,

Dublin, 23d Auguft, 1779.

IF there is any fuch permanent caufe, from which the frequent diftreffes of fo confiderable a part of the Britifh empire have arifen, it is of the utmoft confequence that it fhould be fully explained, and generally underftood. Let us endeavour to trace it by its effects; thefe will manifeftly appear by an attentive review of the ftate of Ireland at different periods.

From the time that king James the Firft had eftablifhed a regular adminiftration of

juftice

juſtice in every part of the kingdom, until the rebellion of 1641, which takes in a period of between thirty and forty years, the growth of Ireland was confiderable *. In the act recognizing the title of king James, the Lords and Commons acknowledge " that many bleffings and benefits had, " within thefe few years paſt, been poured " upon this realm † ;" and at the end of the parliament in 1615, the commons return thanks for the extraordinary pains taken for the good of this republic, whereby they fay " we all of us fit under our own vines, " and the whole realm reapeth the happy " fruits of peace ‡." In his reign the little that could be given by the people, was given with general confent § : and received with extraordinary marks of royal favour; he

---

* Its tranquillity was fo well eſtabliſhed in 1611, that king James reduced his army in Ireland to 176 horfe, and 1450 foot. Additional judges were appointed; circuits eſtabliſhed throughout the kingdom, 2d Cox, 17 ; and Sir John Davis obferves, that no nation under the fun loves equal and indifferent juſtice better than the Iriſh. Davis, p. 184, 166.

† 13 Jac. ch. i.   ‡ 1 Vol. Com. Journ. p. 92.

§ Ib. 61.

he defires the lord-deputy to return them thanks for their fubfidy, and for their granting it with univerfal confent* ; and to affure them that he holds his fubjects of that kingdom in equal favour with thofe of his other kingdoms ; and that he will be as careful to provide for their profperous and flourifhing ftate, as for his own perfon.

Davis, who had ferved him in great ftations in this kingdom, and had vifited every province of it, mentions the profperous ftate of the country, and that the revenue of the crown, both certain and cafual, had been raifed to a double proportion. He takes notice how this was effected, " by the " encouragement given to the maritime " towns and cities, as well to increafe the " trade of merchandize, as to cherifh me- " chanical arts ;" and mentions the confequence, " that the ftrings of this Irifh harp " were all in tune †."

In

---

* 1 Vol. Com. Journ. p. 88.
† Davis, p. 1, 193, 194.

In the fucceeding reign, Ireland for fourteen or fifteen years appears to have greatly advanced in profperity. The commons granted in the feffion of 1634, fix entire fubfidies, which they agreed fhould amount in the collection to 250,000l.*; and the free gifts previoufly given to king Charles the Firft, at different times, amounted to 310,000l.†; in the feffion of 1639, they gave four entire fubfidies, and the clergy eight ; the cuftoms which had been farmed at 500l. yearly, in the beginning of this reign, were in the progrefs of it fet for 54,000l.

The commodities exported were twice as much in value, as the foreign merchandize imported, and fhipping is faid to have increafed an hundred fold §. Their parliament was encouraged to frame laws conducive

* Cox's Hift. of Ireland, 2 Vol. 61.   † Ib.
† Some of thefe fubfides, from the fubfequent times of confufion, were not raifed.
‡ Cox, 2d Vol. p. 33.
§ Leland's Hift. of Ireland, 3d Vol. p. 41.

cive to the happinefs and profperity of themfelves and their pofterities, for the enacting
and "confummating" whereof the king
paffes his royal word; and affures his fubjects of Ireland that they were equally of as
much refpect and dearnefs to him as any
others *.

In the fpeaker's fpeech in 1639, when he
was offered for approbation to the lord-
deputy, he mentions the free and happy
condition of the people of Ireland; fets
forth the particulars ; and in enumerating
the national bleffings, mentions as one,
" that our in-gates and out-gates do ftand
open for trade and traffic †;" and as the
lord chancellor declared his excellency's
" high liking of this oration," it may be
confidered as a fair account of the condition
of Ireland at that time. When the commons had afterwards caught the infection of
the times, and were little difpofed to pay

C   com-

* Lord Strafford's Letters, 2d Vol. p. 297.
† Ir. Com. Journ. 1ft Vol. p. 228, 229.

compliments, they acknowledge, that this kingdom, when the earl of Strafford obtained the government, " was in a flourifhing, " wealthy and happy eftate *."

After the reftoration, from the time that the acts of fettlement and explanation had been fully carried into execution, to the year 1688, Ireland made great advances, and continued, for feveral years, in a moft profperous condition †. Lands were every where improved; rents were doubled ; the kingdom abounded with money; trade flourifhed to the envy of our neighbours ; cities increafed exceedingly ; many places of the kingdom

* Lord Clarendon.   Cox, ib.   Ir. Com. Journ. 1 Vol. p. 280, 311.

† Archbifhop King, in his State of the Proteftants of Ireland, p. 52, 53, 445, 446.   Lord Chief Juftice Keating's Addrefs to James the Second, and his Letter to Sir John Temple, ib.

The prohibition of the exportation of our cattle to England, though a great, was but a temporary diftrefs; and in its confequences greatly promoted the general welfare of this country.

kingdom equalled the improvements of
England ; the king's revenue increafed proportionably to the advance of the kingdom, which was every day growing, and
was *well eftablifhed in plenty and wealth* *; manufactures were fet on foot in divers parts ;
the meaneft inhabitants were at once en-
riched and civilized : and this kingdom is
then reprefented to be the moft improved
and improving fpot of ground in Europe. I
repeat the words of perfons of high rank,
great character and fuperior knowledge, who
could not be deceived themfelves, and were
incapable of deceiving others.

In the former of thefe periods, parliaments were feldom convened in Ireland ;
in the latter, they were fufpended for the
fpace of twenty-fix years ; during that
time the Englifh minifters frequently fhewed
difpofitions unfavourable to the profperity of this kingdom ; and in the interval

between

---

* Lord Sydney's words in his fpeech from the throne,
in 1692, from his own former knowledge of this country.
Ir. Com. Journ. 2d Vol. p. 577.

between thofe two periods, it had been
laid wafte, and almoft depopulated by civil
rage and religious fury. And yet, after being
bleffed with an internal peace of ninety
years, and with a fucceffion of five excellent
fovereigns, who were moft juftly the objects
of our affection and gratitude, and to whom
the people of this country were defervedly
dear; after fo long and happy an intercourfe
of protection grace and favour from the
crown, and of duty and loyalty from the
fubjects, it would be difficult to find any
fubfequent period where fo flattering a view
has been given of the induftry and profperity
of Ireland.

The caufe of this profperity fhould be
mentioned. James, the firft duke of Ormond,
whofe memory fhould be ever revered by
every friend of Ireland, to heal the wound
that this country had received by the prohibition of the export of her cattle to England, obtained from Charles the Second a
letter *, dated the 23d of March 1667, by
which

* Carte, 2 Vol. p. 342, 344.

which he directed that all reftraints upon the exportation of commodities, of the growth or manufacture of Ireland, to foreign parts, fhould be taken off, but not to interfere with the plantation laws, or the charters to the trading companies, and that this fhould be notified to his fubjects of this kingdom; which was accordingly done by a proclamation from the lord lieutenant and council; and at the fame time, by his majefty's permiffion, they prohibited the importation from Scotland of linen, woollen, and other manufactures and commodities, as drawing large fums of money out of Ireland, and a great hindrance to its manufactures. His grace fuccefsfully executed his fchemes of national improvement, having by his own conftant attention, the exertion of his extenfive influence, and the moft princely munificence, greatly advanced the woollen, and revived § the linen manufactures, which England

§ Lord Strafford laid the foundation of the linen manufacture in Ireland, but the troubles which foon after broke out had entirely ftopped the progrefs of it.

England then encouraged in this kingdom, as a compenfation for the lofs of that trade of which fhe had deprived ; it and this encouragement, from that time to the revolution, had greatly increafed the wealth and promoted the improvement of Ireland.

The tyranny and perfecuting policy of James the fecond † after his arrival in Ireland, ruined its trade and revenue; the many great oppreffions which the people fuffered during the revolution had occafioned almoft the *utter defolation* of the country. §   But the nation muft have been reftored in the reign of William to a confiderable degree of ftrength and vigor: their exertions in raifing fupplies to a great amount, from the year 1692 to the year 1698, are fome proof of it. They taxed their goods, their lands, their perfons, in fupport of a prince whom they juftly called their deliverer and defender, and

---

† Harris's Life of K. W. 116.
§ The Words of Lord Sydney, in his fpeech from the throne in 1692. Com. Jour. 2 Vol. 576.

and of a government on which their own
prefervation depended. Thofe fums were
granted †, not only without murmur, but
with the utmoft chearfulnefs, and without
any complaint of the inability, or reprefentation of the diftreffed ftate of the country.

The money brought in for the army at
the revolution, gave life to all bufinefs, and
much fooner than could have been expected
retrieved the affairs of Ireland. This money furnifhed capitals for carrying on the
manufactures of the kingdom. Our exports
increafed in 96, 97 and 98, and our imports
did not rife in proportion, which occafioned a
great balance in our favour; and this increafe
was owing principally to the woollen manufacture. In the laft of thofe years the bal-
lance in favour of Ireland in the account of
exports and imports was 419,442l §.

But in the latter end of this reign the political horizon was overcaft, the national growth
was checked, and the national vigor and induftry

† Ir. Com. Jour. 3 Vol. 45 and 65, that great fupplies
were given during this period.   § Dobbs, p. 5, 6, 7, 19.

duftry impaired by the law made in England, reftraining, in fact prohibiting the exportation of all woollen manufactures from Ireland. From the time of this prohibition no parliament was held in Ireland until the year 1703. Five years were fuffered to pafs before any opportunity was given to apply a remedy to the many evils which fuch a prohibition muft neceffarily have occafioned. The linen-trade was then not thoroughly eftablifhed in Ireland; the woollen manufacture was the ftaple trade, and wool the principal material of that kingdom. The confequences of this prohibition appear in the feffion of 1703 †. The commons § lay before queen Anne a moft affecting reprefentation, containing, to ufe their own words "a true ftate of our deplorable condition," protefting that no groundlefs difcontent was the motive for that application, but a deep fenfe of the evil ftate of their country, and of the farther mifchiefs they have reafon to fear will

fall

† Com. Jour. 3 Vol. 45.
§ Ir. Com. Jour. 3 Vol. 65, 66.

fall upon it, if not timely prevented. They
fet forth the vaft decay and lofs of its trade,
its being almoft exhaufted of coin, that they
are hindered from earning their livelihoods,
and from maintaining their own manufactures, that their poor are thereby become
very numerous; that great numbers of
proteftant families have been conftrained to
remove out of the kingdom, as well into
Scotland as into the dominions of foreign
princes and ftates, and that their foreign
trade and its returns are under fuch reftrictions and difcouragements as to be then become in a manner impracticable, although
that kingdom had by its blood and treafure
contributed to fecure the plantation trade to
the people of England.

In a further addrefs to the queen *, laid
before the duke of Ormond, then lord lieutenant, by the houfe with its fpeaker, they
mention the diftreffed condition of that kingdom, and more efpecially of the induftrious

proteftants,

* Com. Jour. 3 Vol. 149.

proteftants, by the almoft total lofs of trade
and decay of their manufactures, and to
preferve the country from utter ruin, apply
for liberty to export their linen manufactures
to the plantations.

In a fubfequent part of this feffion *, the
commons refolve, that by reafon of the great
decay of trade and difcouragement of the manufactures of this kingdom, many poor tradef-
men were reduced to extreme want and beggary. This refolution was *nem. con.* and the
fpeaker, Mr. Broderick, then his majefty's foli-
citor general, and afterwards lord chancellor,
in his fpeech at the end of the feffion†, informs
the lord lieutenant, that the reprefentation
of the commons was, as to the matters con-
tained in it, the unanimous voice and confent of a very full houfe, and that the foft
and gentle terms ufed by the commons in laying the diftreffed condition of the kingdom
before his majefty, fhewed that their complaints proceeded not from queruloufnefs,
                                                but

* Ir. Com. Jour. 3 Vol. p. 195.   Ib. 207, 208.

but from a neceſſity of feeking redrefs; he adds, " it is to be hoped they may be al-"lowed fuch a proportion of trade, that "they may recover from the great poverty "they now lie under;" and in prefenting the bill of fupply fays, the commons have granted it "in time of extreme poverty." The impoveriſhed ſtate of Ireland, at that time, appears in the fpeech from the throne at the conclufion of the feffion, in which it is mentioned that the commons could not then provide for what was owing to the civil and military lifts *.

The fupply given for two years, commencing at Michaelmas 1703 †, was a fum not exceeding 150,000l. which, confidering that no parliament was held in Ireland fince the year 1698, is at the rate of 30,000l.——— yearly commencing in 1699, and ending in the year 1705.

The great diftrefs of Ireland, from the year 1699, to the year 1703, and the caufe of that diftrefs, cannot be doubted.

Let

* Com. Jour. 3 Vol. p. 210.   † Ib. 79, 94.

Let it now be confidered, whether the fame caufe has operated fince the year 1703. In the year 1704* it appears, that the commons were not able, from the circumftances of the nation at that time, to make provifion for repairing the neceffary fortifications; or for arms and ammunition for the public fafety: and the difficulties which the kingdom then laboured under, and the decay of trade appear by the addreffes of the commons† to the queen, and to the duke of Ormond, then lord lieutenant, who was well acquainted with the ftate of this country; by the queen's anfwer‡, and the addrefs of thanks for it,

In the year 1707 §, the revenue was deficient for payment of the army, and defraying the charges of government; and the commons promife to fupply the deficiency " as far as the prefent circumftances of the " nation will allow."

In

---

* Com. Jour. 3 Vol. p. 298.   † Ib. 225, 266.
‡ Ib. 253, 258.   § Ib. 364, 368, 369.

In 1709, it appears * by the unanimous addrefs of the commons to the lord lieutenant,
that the kingdom was in an impoverifhed
and exhaufted ftate: in 1711 †, they exprefs their approbation of the frugality of
the queen's adminiftration, by which their
expences were leffened, and by that means
the kingdom preferved from taxes, which
might have proved too weighty and burthen-
fome.   In their addrefs to the lord lieutenant, at the clofe of the feffion, they requeft, that he fhould reprefent to her majefty, that they had given all the fupplies
which her majefty defired, and which they, in
their prefent condition, were able to grant ‡:
and yet thofe fupplies amounted, for two
years, to a fum not exceeding 167,023l.
8s. 5d §; though powder magazines, the council chamber, the treafury office, and other
offices were then to be built.

From the fhort parliament of 1713, nothing can be collected, but that the houfe
was

.* Com. Jour. 3 Vol. p. 573.   † Ib. 827.   ‡ Ib. 929.
§ Ib. 876.

was inflamed and divided by party diffentions, and that the fear of danger to the
fucceffion of the prefent illuftrious family,
excluded every other confideration from the
minds of the majority.

This laft period, from the year 1699 to
the death of queen Anne, is marked with the
ftrongeft circumftances of national diftrefs
and defpondency. The reprefentatives of
the people, who were the beft judges, and
feveral of whom were members of the houfe
of commons before and after thefe reftraints, have affigned the reafon. No other
can be affigned.

That the woollen manufactures were the
great fource of induftry in Ireland, appears
from the Irifh ftatute of the 17th and
18th of Charles II. ch. 15*; from the re-
folutions

* In the fame feffion an act was made for the advancement of the linen manufacture, which fhews that both
kingdoms then thought (for thefe laws came to us through
England) that each of thefe manufactures was to be encouraged in Ireland.

folutions of the commons in 1695*, for regulating thofe manufactures; the refoluti-
ons of the committee of fupply in that fef-
fion†; and from the preamble to the Englifh
ftatute of the 10th and 11th of William III.
ch. 10; in which it is recited, that great
quantities of thofe manufactures were made,
and were daily increafing in Ireland, and
were exported from thence to foreign markets.

Of the exportation of all thofe manufactures the Irifh were at once totally deprived:
the linen manufacture, propofed as a fub-
ftitute, muft have required the attention of
many years before it could be thoroughly
eftablifhed. What muft have been the confequences to Ireland in the mean time? the
journals of the commons in queen Anne's
reign have informed us. Compare this period with the three former, and you will
prove this melancholy truth; that a country

* Ir. Com. Jour. 2 Vol. p. 725.   † Ib. 733.

try will fooner recover from the miferies and devaftation occafioned by war, invafion, rebellion, maffacre, than from laws reftraining the commerce, difcouraging the manufactures, fettering the induftry, and above all breaking the fpirits of the people.

It would be injuftice not to acknowledge that Great Britain has, for a long feries of years, made great exertions to repair the evils arifing from thefe reftraints. She has opened her great markets to part of the linen manufacture of Ireland; fhe has encouraged it by granting, for a great length of time, large fums of her own money † on the exportation of it; and under her protection, and by the perfevering induftry of our people, this manufacture has attained to a great degree of perfection and profperity, in fome parts of this country. If the kind and conftant attention of that great kingdom, with

† The fums paid on the exportation of Irifh linens from Great Britain, at a medium of twenty-nine years, from 1743 to 1773, amount to fomething under 10,000l. yearly.—Ir. Com. Jour. 16 Vol. p. 374, the account returned from the infpector general's office in Great Britain.

with which we are connected to this important object; or if the lenient courfe of time
had at length healed thofe wounds, which
commercial jealoufy had given to the trade
and induftry of this country, it would not
be a friendly hand to either kingdom that
would attempt to open them: but, if upon
every accident they bleed anew, they fhould
be carefully examined, and fearched to the
bottom. If the caufe of the poverty and
diftrefs of Ireland in the reign of queen
Anne has fince continued to operate, though
not always in fo great a degree, yet fufficient
frequently to reduce to mifery, and con-
ftantly to check the growth and impair the
ftrength of that kingdom, and to weaken
the force and to reduce the refources of
Great Britain ; that man ought to be confidered as a friend to the Britifh empire,
who endeavours to eftablifh this important truth, and to explain a fubject fo
little underftood. If in this attempt there
fhall appear no intention to raife jealoufies,
inflame difcontents, or agitate conftitutional
queftions, it is hoped that thofe letters may

D   be

be read without prejudice on one fide of the water, and without paffion or refentment on the other.

I have the honour to be, my lord, &c.

THE

THE

COMMERCIAL RESTRAINTS

OF

IRELAND

CONSIDERED.

THIRD LETTER.

D 2

THE

COMMERCIAL RESTRAINTS

O F

I R E L A N D

C O N S I D E R E D.

T H I R D   L E T T E R.

My Lord,

Dublin, 25th Auguſt, 1779.

To an inquirer after truth, hiſtory ſince the year 1699 furniſhes very imperfect and often partial views of the affairs of Great Britain and Ireland. The latter has no profeſſed hiſtorian of its own ſince that æra, and is ſo ſlightly mentioned in the hiſtories of the former kingdom, that it ſeems to be introduced rather to ſhew the accuracy of the accomptant, than as an article to be read and examined; pamphlets are often written to ſerve occaſional purpoſes, and with an intention to miſrepreſent; and party writers

ters are not worthy of any regard. We
muſt then endeavour to find ſome other
guide, and look into the beſt materials for
hiſtory, by conſidering the facts as recorded
in the journals of parliament; theſe have
evinced the poverty of Ireland for the firſt
fourteen years of this century. That this
poverty continued in the year 1716, appears
by the unanimous addreſs of the houſe of
commons to George the Firſt*. This addreſs
was to congratulate his majeſty on his ſuc-
ceſs in extinguiſhing the rebellion, an occaſion moſt joyful to them, and on which no
diſagreeable circumſtance would have been
ſtated, had not truth and the neceſſities of
their country extorted it from them. A
ſmall debt of 16,106l. 11s. o½d. †, due at Michaelmas 1715, was, by their exertions to
ſtrengthen the hands of government in that
year, increaſed at Midſummer 1717 to a
ſum of 91537l. 17s. 1⅝d. §, which was conſidered as ſuch an augmentation of the national

* Com. Jour. 4 Vol. p. 249,   † Ib. 296.
§ Ib. 335.

tional debt, that the lord lieutenant, the duke of Bolton, thought it neceffary to take notice in his fpeech from the throne, that the debt was confiderably augmented, and to declare at the fame time that his majefty had ordered reductions in the military, and had thought proper to leffen the civil lift.

There cannot be a ftronger proof of the want of refources in any country, than that a debt of fo fmall an amount fhould alarm the perfons intrufted with the government of it. That thofe apprehenfions were well founded, will appear from the repeated diftreffes of Ireland, from time to time, for many years afterwards. In 1721, the fpeech from the throne *, and the addreffes to the king and to the lord lieutenant, ftate, in the ftrongeft terms, the great decay of her trade, and the very low and impoverifhed ftate to which fhe was reduced.

That

* Com. Jour. 4 Vol. p. 694, 700, 701.

That this procceded, in fome meafure, from calamities and misfortunes which af- fected the neighbouring kingdoms, is true: but their effects on Ireland, little interefted in the South Sea project, could not be con- fiderable. The poverty under which fhe laboured, arofe principally from her own fituation: The lord lieutenant fays there is ground to hope that in this feffion fuch remedies may be applied, as will reftore the nation to a flourifhing condition; and the commons return the king thanks for giving them that opportunity to confider of the beft methods for reviving their decayed trade, and making them a flourifhing and happy people.

But it is a melancholy proof of the defpond- ing ftate of this kingdom, that no law what- ever was then propofed for encouraging trade or manufactures, or to follow the words of the addrefs, for reviving trade, or making us a flourifhing people, unlefs that for amend- ing the laws as to butter and tallow cafks de- ferves to be fo called; and why? becaufe it

was

was well underftood by both houfes of parliament that they had no power to remove
thofe reftraints which prohibited trade and
difcouraged manufactures, and that any application for that purpofe would at that time
have only offended the people on one fide of
the channel, without bringing any relief to
thofe on the other. The remedy propofed by
government, and partly executed, by directing
a commiffion under the great feal for receiving
· voluntary fubfcriptions *, in order to eftablifh
a bank, was a fcheme to circulate paper
without money; and confidering that it
came fo foon after the fouth fea bubble had
burft, it is more furprifing that it fhould
have been at firft applauded †, than that it
was in the fame feffion difliked, cenfured and
abandoned §. The total inefficacy of the
remedy proved however the inveteracy of
the difcafe, and furnifhes a farther proof of
the defperate fituation of Ireland, when
nothing could be thought of for its relief, but
that

* Ir. Com. Jour. 4 Vol. p. 694.   † Ib. 720.
§ Ib. 832.

that paper fhould circulate without money,
trade or manufactures *.

In the following feffion of 1723, it appears
that the condition of our manufacturers,
and of the loweft claffes of our people, muft
have been diftreffed, as the duke of Graf-
ton, in his fpeech from the throne, particularly recommends to their confideration the
finding out of fome method for the better
employing of the poor †; and though the
debt of the nation was no more than
66,318l. 8s. 3½d. ‡ and was lefs than in the
laft feffion §, yet the commons thought it
neceffary to prefent an addrefs to the king,
to give fuch directions as he, in his great
goodnefs fhould think proper, to prevent
the increafe of the debt of the nation. This
addrefs was prefented ‖ by the houfe, with
its

---

* It is not here intended to enter into the queftion, whether in different circumftances a national bank might not
be ufeful to Ireland.

† Com. Jour. 5 Vol. p. 12.   ‡ 5 Vol. p. 102.

§ It was then 77,261l. 6s. 7 d. 4 Vol. p. 778.

‖ Ib. 108.

its fpeaker, and paffed *nem. con.* and was occafioned by the diftreffed ftate of the country, and by their apprehenfions that it
might be further exhaufted by the projeĉt of
Woods's half-pence : it could not be meant
as any want of refpeĉt to their lord lieutenant, as they had not long fince returned
him thanks for his wife conduĉt and frugality in not increafing the debt of the nation*;
this addrefs of the commons, and the lord
lieutenant's recommendation for the better
employing the poor, feems to be explained
by a petition of the woollen-drapers, weavers
and clothiers of the city of Dublin, (the
principal feat of the woollen manufaĉture of
Ireland) in behalf of themfelves and the other
drapers, weavers and clothiers of this kingdom, praying relief in relation to the great
decay of trade in the woollen manufacture †.

But this addrefs had no effeĉt ; the debt
of the nation in the enfuing feffion of 1725,

was

* Com. Jour. 4 Vol. p. 16.   † Ib. 136.

was nearly doubled*; in the fpeeches from the throne in 1727, Lord Carteret takes notice of our fuccefs in the linen trade, and yet obferves in 1729, that the revenue had fallen fhort, and that thereby a confiderable arrear was due to the eftablifhment.

But notwithftanding the fuccefs of the linen manufacture †, Ireland was in a moft miferable condition. The great fcarcity of corn had been fo univerfal in this kingdom in the years 1728 and 1729, as to expofe thoufands of families to the utmoft neceffities, and even to the danger of famine; many artificers and houfe-keepers having been obli ed to beg for bread in the ftreets of Dublin. It appeared before the houfe of commons that the import of corn for one year and fix months, ending the 29th dayof September, 1729, amounted in value to. the fum of 274,000l. an amazing fum compared with the circumftances of the kingdom at.

---

* At midfummer, 1725, it amounted to 119,215l. 5s.]
3d. 5 Vol. Com. Jour. p. 282, 295. Ib. 434, 435, 642.
† Ib. 732, 755.

at that time! and the commons refolve that public granaries would greatly contribute to the increafing of tillage, and providing againft fuch wants as have frequently befallen the people of this kingdom, and hereafter may befall them, unlefs proper precautions fhall be taken againft fo great a calamity.

The great fcarcity which happened in the years 28 and 29, and frequently before and fince, is a decifive proof that the diftreffes of this kingdom have been occafioned by the difcouragement of manufactures; if the manufacturers have not fufficient employment they cannot buy the fuperfluous produce of the land; the farmers will be difcouraged from tilling, and general diftrefs and poverty muft enfue. The confequences of the want of employment among manufacturers and labourers muft be more fatal in Ireland than in moft other countries; of the numbers of her people it has been computed that 1,887,220 live in houfes with but one hearth, and may therefore be reafonably prefumed

prefumed to belong, for the moft part, to thofe claffes.

In the year 1731 * there was a great defi-ciency in the public revenue, and the natio-nal debt had confiderably increafed. The ex-haufted kingdom lay under great difficulties by the decay of trade, the fcarcity of money and the univerfal poverty of the country, which the fpeaker reprefents § in very affec-ting terms, in offering the money-bills for the royal affent, and adds, "that the com-" mons hope from his majefty's goodnefs, " and his grace's *free* and *impartial* reprefen-" tation of the ftate and condition of this " kingdom, that *they* may enjoy a *fhare* of " the bleffings of public tranquillity, by the " increafe of their trade and the encourage-" ment of their manufactures."

But in the next feffion, of 1733, they are told in the fpeech from the throne, what this fhare was to be. The lord lieutenant in-forms

* Duke of Dorfet's fpeech from the throne, Com. Jour,
6 Vol. p. 12.   § Ib. 143.

forms them that the peace cannot fail of
contributing to their welfare, by enabling
them to improve thofe branches of trade and
manufactures † which *are properly their own*,
meaning the trade and manufacture of linen.
Whether this idea of property has been preferved inviolate will hereafter appear.

The years 40 and 41 were feafons of great
fcarcity, and in confequence of the want of
wholefome provifions great numbers of our
people perifhed miferably, and the fpeech
from the throne recommends it to both
houfes to confider of proper meafures to prevent the like calamity for the future. The
employment of the poor and the encouragement of tillage, are the remedies propofed §
by the lord lieutenant and approved of by
the commons, but no laws for thofe purpofes were introduced, and why they were not
affords matter for melancholy conjecture.
They could not have been infenfible of the
miferies of their fellow-creatures; many
thoufands

† Com. Jour. 6 v. 189.
§ 7 V. Com. Jour. 214, 220, 222.

thoufands of whom were loft in thofe years, fome from abfolute want, and many from diforders occafioned by bad provifions. Why was no attempt made for their relief? becaufe the commons knew that the evil was out of their reach, that the poor were not employed becaufe they were difcouraged by reftrictive laws from working up the materials of their own country, and that agriculture could not be encouraged where the lower claffes of the people were not enabled by their induftry to purchafe the produce of the farmer's labour.

For above forty years after making thofe reftrictive laws * Ireland was always poor and often in great want, diftrefs and mifery, § tho' the linen manufacture had made great progrefs during that time. In the war before the laft, fhe was not able to give any affiftance. The duke of Devonfhire, in the year 1741, takes

---

* The act intitled an act for better regulation of partrerfhips, and to encourage the trade and manufactures of this kingdom, has not a word relative to the latter part of the title.

§ Com. Jour. 6 v. 694, 7 v. 742.

takes notice from the throne, that during a war for the protection of the trade of all his majefty's dominions there had been no increafe of the charge of the eftablifhment; and in the year 1745 the country was fo little able to bear expence, that lord Chefterfield difcouraged and prevented any augmentation of the army, tho' much defired by many gentlemen of the houfe of commons, from a fenfe of the great danger that then impended. An influx of money after the peace, and the further fuccefs of the linen trade, encreafed our wealth, and enabled us to reduce by degrees, and afterwards to difcharge the national debt. This was not effected until the firft of March 1754*. This debt was occafioned principally by the expences incurred by the rebellion in Great Britain in the year 1715; an unlimited vote

E   of

* The fum remaining due on the loans at lady-day 1753 was 85,585l 0s 0½d The whole credit of the nation to that day was 332,747l. 19s 1½d and, deducting the fums due on the loans, amounted to 247,162l 18s 3½d. Com. Jour. 9 v. 3, 349, 352.

of credit was then given §. From the lownefs
of the revenue, and the want of refources,
not from any further exertions on the part
of the kingdom in point of expence, the
debt of 16,106l 11s 0½d due in 1715, was
encreafed at Lady Day† 1733, to 371,312l
12s 2½d. That government and the houfe
of commons fhould for fuch a length of
time have confidered the reduction and difcharge of this debt as an object of fo great
importance, and that near forty years fhould
have paffed, before the conftant attention and
ftricteft œconomy of both could have accom-
plifhed that purpofe, is a ftrong proof of the
weaknefs and poverty of this country, during that period.

After the payment of this debt, the wealth
and ability of Ireland were greatly overrated, both here and in Great Britain. The
confequences of this miftaken opinion were
encreafed expences on the part of government

§ Com. Jour. vol. 4. 195.
† Com. Jour, vol. 6. 289.

ment and of the country, more than it was
able to bear. The ſtrict œconomy of old
times was no longer practiſed. The reprefentatives of the people ſet the example of
profuſion, and the miniſters of the crown
were not backward in following it. A large
redundency of money in the treaſury, gave
a deluſive appearance of national wealth.
At Lady Day 1755 the ſum in credit to the
nation.was 471,404l 5s 6d¾ ‖, and the money
remaining in the treaſury of the ordinary
unappropriated revenue on the 29th day of
September 1755*, 457,959l 12s 7d⅓. But this
great increaſe of revenue aroſe from an increaſe of imports, particularly in the year
1754, by which the kingdom was greatly o-
verſtocked, and which raiſed the revenue in
that year 208,309l 19s 2d⅓ higher than it
was in the year 1748, when the revenue
firſt began to riſe conſiderably †; and though
what a nation ſpends is one method of eſti-
mating its wealth, yet a nation, like an indi-
E 2 vidual,

‖ Com. Jour. 9 v. 352.   * Ib. 331.
† Com. Jour. 10 Vol. 751.

vidual, may live beyond its means, and fpend on credit which may far exceed its income. This was the fact as to Ireland in the year 1754, for fome years before and for many years after; it appeared in an enquiry before the houfe of commons in the feffion of 1755, that many perfons had circulated paper to a very great amount, far exceeding not only their own capitals *, but that juft proportion which the quantity of paper ought to bear to the national fpecie. This gave credit to many individuals, who without property be-came merchant importers, and at the fame time increafed the receipts of the treafury and leffened the wealth of the kingdom. At the very time that fo great a balance was in the treafury, public credit was in a very low way, and the houfe of commons was employed in preparing a law to reftore it. In 54 and 55 three principal banks‡ had failed,

---

* Com. Jour. 9 v. 818.   † Ib. 819, 829, 846, 865.

‡ March 6, 1754, Thomas Dillon and Richard Ferral, failed. 3d March 1755, William Lennox and George French. Same day John Wilcocks and John Dawfon.

failed and the legiflature took up much time in enquiring into their affairs, and in framing laws for the relief of their creditors §. Yet in this feffion, the liberality of the houfe of commons was exceffive. The redundency in the treafury had in the feffion of 1753, occafioned a difpute between the crown and the houfe of commons on the queftion, whether the king's previous confent was neceffary for the application of it. They wifhed to avoid any future conteft of that kind, and were flattered to grant the public money from enlarged views of national improvements. The making rivers navigable, the making and improving harbours, and the improvement of hufbandry and other ufeful arts, were objects worthy of the reprefentatives of the people; and had the faithfulnefs of the execution anfwered the goodnefs of the intention in many inftances, the public in general might have had no great reafon to complain. Many of thofe grants prove the poverty of the country.

There

§ There was then no Bankruptcy law in Ireland.

There were not private ftocks to carry on
the projeacts of individuals, nor funds fufficient for incorporating and fupporting companies, nor profits to be had by the under-
takings fufficient to reimburfe the money
neceffary to be expended. The commons
therefore advanced the money, for the benefit of the public; and it can never be fuppofed that they would have continued to
do fo for above twenty years, if they
were not convinced that there were not
funds in the hands of individuals fufficient to carry on thofe ufeful undertak-
ings, nor trade enough in the kingdom
to make adequate returns to the adventurers.

Having gone through more than half
the century, it is time to paufe. In this
long gloomy period, the poverty of Ireland appears to have been mifery and
defolation, and her wealth a fymptom of
decline and a prelude to poverty; the low
retiring ebb from the fpring-tide of deceitful

ceitful profperity, has left our fhores bare,
and has opened a wafte and defolate prof-
pect of barren fand, and uncultivated country.

I have the honour to be,

My lord, &c.

THE

THE

COMMERCIAL RESTRAINTS

OF

IRELAND

CONSIDERED.

FOURTH LETTER.

THE

COMMERCIAL RESTRAINTS

OF

IRELAND

CONSIDERED.

FOURTH LETTER.

MY LORD,

Dublin, 27th Auguſt, 1779.

THE revenue, for the reaſons already giv-
en, decreaſed in 1755†, fell lower in 1756,
and ſtill lower in 57. In the laſt year the
vaunted proſperity of Ireland was changed
into miſery and diſtreſs; the lower claſſes of
our people wanted food*; the money ariſing
from

† Com. Jour. 10 v. 751.
* Ib. 10 v. 16. Speech from the throne, and ib. 25,
addreſs from the houſe of commons to the king.

from the extravagance of the rich was freely applied to alleviate the fufferings of the
poor ‡. One of the firft fteps of the late
duke of Bedford's adminiftration, and which
reflects honour on his memory, was obtaining a king's letter, dated 3ıft March 1757,
for 20,cool to be laid out as his grace fhould
think the moft likely to afford the moft
fpeedy and effectual relief to his majefty's
poor fubjects of this kingdom. His grace,
in his fpeech from the throne, humanely
expreffes his wifh, that fome method might
be found out to prevent the calamities that
are the confequences of a want. of corn,
which had been in part felt the laft year,
and to which this country had been too often expofed; the commons acknowledge
that thofe calamities had been frequently
and were too fenfibly and fatally experienced in the courfe of the laft year, thank
his grace for his early and charitable attention to the neceffities of the poor of this
country in their late diftreffes, and make
ufe of thofe remarkable expreffions, " that
" they

‡ Com. Jeur. 10 vol. p. 25, Addrefs from the houfe of
commons to the king.

" they will moſt chearfully embrace‡ every " *practicable* method to promote tillage †, They knew that the encouragement of manufactures were the effectual means, and that theſe means were not in their power.

The ability of the nation was eſtimated by the money in the treaſury, and the penſions on the civil eſtabliſhment, excluſive of French, which at Lady-day 1755, were 38,003l. 15s. od. amounted at Lady-day 57, to 49,293l. 15s. od §.

The ſame ideas were entertained of the reſources of this country in the ſeſſion of 1759. Great Britain had made extraordinary

‡ Com. Jour. 1Q vol. 25.

† They brought in a law for the enccuragement of tillage, which was ineffectual (ſee poſt 42) but the preamble of that act is a legiſlative proof of the unhappy condition of the poor of this country before that time. The preamble recites, " the *extreme* neceſſity to which the poor " of this kingdom had been too frequently reduced for " want of proviſions."

§ Com. Jour. 10 vol. 285.

nary efforts, and engaged in enormous expences for the protection of the whole empire. This country was in immediate danger of an invafion. Every Irifhman was
agreed that fhe fhould affift Great Britain to
the utmoft of her ability, but this ability
was too highly eftimated. The nation a-
bounded rather in loyalty than in wealth †.
Our brethren in Great Britain, had, however,
formed a different opinion, and furveying
their own ftrength, were incompleat judges
of our weaknefs. A lord lieutenant of too
much virtue and magnanimity to fpeak
what he did not think, takes notice from the
throne, " of the profperous ftate of this
" country, improving daily in its manufactures and commerce‖." His grace had done
much to bring it to that ftate, by obtaining
for us fome of the beft laws * in our books
of ftatutes. But this part of the fpeech was
not taken notice of, either in the addrefs

to

† 11 V. 472, Speaker's fpeech.   ‖ 11 V. 16.
* The acts paffed in 58, giving bounties on the land-
carriage of corn, and on coals brought to Dublin.

to his majefty, or to his grace, from a houfc
of commons well-difpofed to give every
mark of duty and refpect, and to pay every
compliment confiftent with truth. The e-
vent proved the wifdom of their referve.
The public expences were greatly increafed,
the penfions on the civil eftablifhment exclufive of French, at Lady-day 1759, a-
mounted to 55,497l. 5s. od.* there was at
the fame time a great augmentation of military expence†. Six new regiments and a
troop were raifed in a very fhort fpace of
time. An unanimous and unlimited addrefs
of confidence to his grace‡, a fpecifick vote
of credit for 150,000l. ‖, which was afterwards provided for in the loan-bill § of that
feffion, a fecond vote of credit in the fame
feffion for 300,000l. **, the raifing the rate of
intereft paid by government, one per cent.
and the payment out of the treafury ++ in
little more than one year, of 703,957l 3s 1½d ‡‡

were

* Com. Jour. 11 Vol. p. 212. † Ib. from 826, to 837.
‡ Vol. 11, p. 141.   ‖ Ib. 408.   § Ib. 473.
** Ib. 862.   ++ Ib.   ‡‡ Ib. 982, from 25th March
59, to 21ft of April 60, exclufive.

were the confequences of thofe encreafed
expences. The effects of thefe exertions
were immediately and feverely felt by the
kingdom. Thefe loans could not be fupplied by a poor country, without draining the
bankers of their cafh; three of the principal houfes* among them ftopped payment;
the three remaining banks in Dublin dif-
counted no paper, and in fact, did no bufinefs. Public and private credit, that had
been drooping fince the year 1754, had now
fallen proftrate. At a general meeting of
the merchants of Dublin, in April 1760,
with feveral members of the houfe of commons, the inability of the former to carry
on bufinefs was univerfally acknowledged,
not from the want of capital, but from the
ftoppage of all paper circulation, and the re-
fufal of the remaining bankers to difcount
the bills even of the firft houfes. The
merchants and traders of Dublin, in their
petition § to the houfe of commons, reprefent

---

* Clements's, Dawfon's and Mitchell's.

§ Com. Jour. 11 Vol. 966. April 15, 1760.

fent " the low ftate to which public and " private credit had been of late reduced in " this kingdom, and particularly in this " city, of which the fucceffive failures of " fo many banks, and of private traders in " different parts of this kingdom, in fo " fhort a time as fince October laft, were " inconteftable proofs. The petitioners, " fenfible that the neceffary confequences " of thefe misfortunes muft be the lofs of " foreign trade, the diminution of his ma- " jefty's revenue, and what is ftill more " fatal, the decay of the manufactures of " this kingdom, have in vain repeatedly " attempted to fupport the finking credit " of the nation by affociations and other- " wife; and are fatisfied that no refource " is now left but what may be expected " from the wifdom of parliament, to avert " the calamities with which this kingdom is " at prefent threatened."

The committee, to whom it was referred, refolve * that they had proved the feveral

F matters

matters alledged in their petition ; that the
quantity of paper circulating was not near
fufficient for fupporting the trade and manufactures of this kingdom ; and that the
houfe fhould engage, to the firft of May 62,
for each of the then fubfifting banks in
Dublin, to the amount of 50,000l. for each
bank ; and that an addrefs fhould be
prefented to the lord lieutenant, to
thank his grace for having given directions
that banker's notes fhould be received as
cafh from the feveral fubfcribers to the loan,
and that he would be pleafed to give directions that their notes fhould be taken as
cafh in all payments at the treafury, and by
the feveral collectors for the city and county
of Dublin. The houfe agreed to thofe re-
folutions, and to that for giving credit to the
banks, *nem. con.*

The fpeech from the throne takes notice
of the care the houfe of commons had taken for eftablifhing public credit, which the
lord lieutenant fays he flatters himfelf will
anfwer the end propofed, and effect that circulation

culation fo neceffary for carrying on the commerce of the country *.

Thofe facts arc not ftated as any imputa-
tion on the then chief governor : the vigour
of his mind incited him to make the crown
as ufeful as poffible to the fubjeft, and the
fubjeft to the crown. He fuccccded in
both , but in the latter part of the experiment the weaknefs of the country was
fhewn. The great law which we owe to his
interpofition, I fpeak of that which gives a
bounty on the land carriage of corn and
flour to Dublin †, has faved this country from
utter deftruftion; this law, which reflects
the higheft honour en the author and pro-
moter, is ftill a proof of the poverty of that
country where fuch a law is neceffary. Its
true principle is to bring the market of Dublin to the door of the farmer, and that was
done in the year ending the 25th of March
1777 at the expence of 617891. 18s. 6d. to
F 2   the

* Com. Jour. 11 Vol. p. 1049.
† Brought in by Mr. Pery, the prefent Speaker.

the public; a large but a moſt uſeful and neceſſary expenditure*. The adoption of this principle proves, what we in this country know to be a certain truth, that there is no other market in Ireland on which the farmer can rely for the certain ſale of his corn and flour; a deciſive circumſtance to ſhew the wretched ſtate of the manufactures of this kingdom.

In the beginning of the next parliament, the rupture with Spain occaſioned a new augmentation of military expence. The ever loyal commons return an addreſs of thanks to the meſſage mentioning the addition of five new battallions†, and unanimouſly promiſe to provide for them; and with the ſame unanimity paſs a vote of credit for 200,000l §. The amount of penſions on the civil eſtabliſhment, excluſive of French,

---

* In the year ending lady-day 1778 it amounted to 71,533l 1s., and in that ending lady-day 1779 to 67864l. 8s. 10d.

† Com. Jour. 12 Vol. p. 700.   § Ib. 728.

French, had for one year ending the 25th
of March 176: amounted to 64,127l. 5s.‡
and our manufacturers were then diftreffed
by the expence and havock of a burthen-
fome war *.

⁚

In the year 1762 a national evil made its
appearance, which all the exertions of the
government and of the legiflature have not
fince been able to eradicate ; I mean the
rifings of the White Boys. They appear in
thofe parts of the kingdom where manufactures are not eftablifhed, and are a proof of
the poverty and want of employment of the
lower claffes of our people. Lord Nor-
thumberland mentions, in his fpeech from
the throne † in 1763, that the means of induftry would be the remedy ; from whence
it feems to follow that the want of thofe
means muft be the caufe. To attain this
great end the commons promife their attention

‡ Com. Journ. 12 Vol. p. 443.
* Ib. 929, Speech of Lord Hallifax from the throne,
30th April, 1762.
† Ir. Com. Journ. 13 Vol. p. 21.

tion to the proteſtant charter ſchools and linen manufacture‡. The wretched men, who were guilty of thoſe violations of the law, were too mature for the firſt, and totally ignorant of the ſecond; but long eſtabliſhed uſage had given thoſe words a privilege in ſpeeches and addreſſes to ſtand for every thing that related to the improvement of Ireland.

The ſtate of penſions remained nearly the ſame*; by the peace the military expences were conſiderably reduced; of the military eſtabliſhment to be provided for in the ſeſſion 1763, compared with the military eſtabliſhment as it ſtood on the 31ſt of March 1763, the net decreaſe was 119,037l. os. 10d. per annum; but as a peace eſtabliſhment it was high, and compared with that of the 31ſt of March 1756 †, being the year preceding

‡ Com. Jour. 13 Vol. p. 23.

* For a year ending 25th March 1763 they were 66,477l. 5s.; they afterwards roſe to 89,095l. 17s. 6d. in September 1777 at the higheſt; and in this year, ending the 25th March laſt, amounted to 85,971l. 2s. 6d.

† Com. Jour. 13 Vol. p. 576.

ceding the laſt war, the annual increaſe was 110,422l. 9s. 5¼d. the debt of the na-tion at lady-day 1763, and which was en-tirely incurred in the laſt war, was 521,161l. 16s. 6¼d.* and would have been much greater if the ſeveral lord lieutenants had not uſed with great œconomy the power of borrowing, which the houſe of commons had from ſeſſion to ſeſſion given them.

That this debt ſhould have been con-tracted in an expenſive war, in which Ire-land was called upon for the firſt time to contribute, is not to be wondered at, but the continual increaſe of this debt, in fix-teen years of peace, ſhould be accounted for.

The ſame miſtaken eſtimate of the abi-lity of Ireland, that occaſioned our being called upon to bear part of the Britiſh burthen during the war, produced ſimilar effects at the time of the peace, and after it.

* Com. Jour. 13 Vol. p. 574, 621.

it. The heavy peace eftablifhment was increafed by an augmentation of our army in
1769, which induced an additional charge,
taking in the expences of exchange and re-
mittance, of 54,118l. 12s. 6d. yearly, for the
firft year ; but this charge was afterwards
confiderably increafed, and amounted from
the year 1769 to Chriftmas 1778, when it
was difcontinued, to the fum of 620,824l. os.
9¼d.; and this increafed expence was more
felt, becaufe it was for the purpofe of paying forces out of this kingdom.

As our expences increafed our income diminifhed ; the revenue for the two years, ending the 25th of March 1771 *, was far fhort
of former years, and not nearly fufficient
to pay the charges of government, and the
fums payable for bounties and public works†.
The debt of the nation at lady-day 1771,
was increafed to 782,320l. os. o¼d‡. The
want of income was endeavoured to be fupplied by a loan. In the money-bill of the
October

* Com. Jour. 14 Vol. p. 715.   † 15 Vol. p. 710.
‡ Ib. p. 153,

October feſſion 1771, there was a clauſe impowering government to borrow 200,000l. Immediately after the linen trade declined rapidly; in 1772, 1773, and 1774, the decay in that trade was general in every part of the kingdom where it was eſtabliſhed; the quantity manufactured was not above two thirds of what uſed formerly to be made, and that quantity did not ſell for above three-fourths of its former price; the linen and linen yarn exported for one year, ending the 25th of March 1773 ‡, fell ſhort of the exports of one year, ending the 25th of March 1771, to the amount in value of 788,821l. 1s. 3d. At lady-day 1773 *, the debt increaſed to 994,890l. 10s. 10½d. The attempt in the feſſion of 1773 †, to equalize the annual income and expences failed, and borrowing on tontine in the feſſions of 1773, 1775 and 1777, added greatly to the annual expence, and to the ſums of money remitted out of the kingdom. The debt now bearing intereſt

‡ Com. Jour. 16 Vol. p. 372.   * Ib. p. 190, 191, 193.
† Ib. 256.

intereft amounts to the fum of 1,017,600l. befides a fum of 740,000l. raifed on annuities, which amount to 48,900l. yearly, with fome incidental expences. The great increafe of thofe national burdens, likely to take place in the approaching feffion, has been already mentioned.

The debt of Ireland has arifen from the following caufes: the expences of the late war, the heavy peace eftablifhment in the year 1763, the increafe of that eftablifh-ment in the year 1769, the fums paid from 1759 to forces out of the kingdom, the great increafe of penfions and other additional charges on the civil eftablifhment, which however confiderable, bears but a fmall proportion to the increafed military expences, the falling of the revenue, and the fums paid for bounties and public works; thefe are mentioned laft, becaufe it is apprehended that they have not operated to increafe this debt in fo great a degree as fome perfons have imagined; for though the amount is large, yet no part of the money

was

was fent out of the kingdom, and feveral of the grants were for ufeful purpofes, fome of which made returns to the public and to the treafury exceeding the amount of thofe grants.   )

When thofe facts are confidered, no doubt can be entertained but that the fup-pofed wealth of Ireland has led to real po-verty ; and when it is known, that from the year 1751 to Chriftmas 1778 the fums, remitted by Ireland to pay troops ferving abroad, amounted to the fum of 1,401,925l. 19s. 4d. it will be equally clear from whence this poverty has principally arifen.

In thofe feafons of expence and borrow-ing, the lower claffes were equally fubject to poverty and diftrefs, as in the periods of na-tional œconomy.   In 1762 lord Hallifax, in his fpeech from the throne*, acknow-ledges that our manufactures were dif-treffed by the war.   In 1763, the corpora-tion

* Com. Jour. 12 Vol. p. 928.

tion of weavers, by a petition to the houfe
of commons, complain that, notwithftanding the great increafe both in number and
wealth of the inhabitants of the metropolis,
they found a very great decay of feveral
very valuable branches of trade and manufactures * of this city, particularly in the
filken and woollen.

In 1765 there was a fcarcity caufed by
the failure of potatoes in general throughout
the kingdom, which diftreffed the common
people; the fpring corn had alfo failed, and
grain was fo high, that it was thought neceffary to appoint a committee + to inquire
what may be the beft method to reduce it;
and to prevent a great dearth, two acts were
paffed early in that feffion, to ftop the dif-
tillery, and to prevent the exportation of
corn, for a limitted time. In fpring 1766
thofe fears appeared to have been well-
founded; feveral towns were in great diftrefs for corn; and by the humanity of the
lord

* Com. Jour. 13 Vol. p. 987.
† Ib. 14 Vol. p. 69, 114, 151.

lord lieutenant, lord Hertford, money was iffued out of the treafury to buy corn for fuch places as applied to his lordfhip for that relief.

The years 1770 and 1771 were feafons of great diftrefs in Ireland, and in the month of February in the latter year, the high price of corn is mentioned from the throne*, as an object of the firft importance, which demanded the utmoft attention.

In 1778 and 1779 there was great plenty of corn, but the manufacturers were not able to buy, and many thoufands of them were fupported by charity; the confequence was that corn fell to fo low a price that the farmers in many places were unable to pay their rents, and every where were under great difficulties.

That the linen manufacture has been of the utmoft confequence to this country, that

* Com. Jour. 14 Vol. p. 665.

that it has greatly profpered, that it has been long encouraged by the protection of Great Britain, that whatever wealth Ireland is poffeffed of arifes, for the moft part, from that trade, is freely acknowledged; but in far the greateft part of the kingdom it has not yet been eftablifhed, and many attempts to introduce it have, after long perfeverance and great expence, proved fruitlefs.

Though that manufacture made great advances from 1727 to 1758 *, yet the tillage of this kingdom declined during the whole of that period, and we have not fince been free from fcarcity.

Notwithftanding the fuccefs of that manufacture, the bulk of our people have always continued poor, and in a great many feafons have wanted food. Can the hiftory of any other fruitful country on the globe, enjoying peace for fourfcore years, and not vifited by plague or peftilence, produce fo

many

* Com. Jour. 16 Vol. p. 467, report from committee, nd ib. 501 agreed to by the houfe, *nem. con.*

many recorded inflances of the poverty and wretchednefs, and of the reiterated want and mifery of the lower orders of the people ? There is no fuch example in ancient or modern ftory. If the ineffectual endeavours by the reprefentatives of thofe poor people to give them employment and food, had not left fufficient memorials of their wretchednefs; if their habitations, apparel, and food were not fufficient proofs, I fhould appeal to the human countenance for my voucher, and reft the evidence on that hopelefs defpondency that hangs on the brow of unemployed induftry.

That fince the fuccefs of the linen manufacture, the money and the rents of Ireland have been greatly increafed, is acknowledged ; but it is affirmed, and the fact is of notoriety, that the lower orders, not of that trade, are not lefs wretched. Thofe employed in the favoured manufacture generally buy from that country to which they principally fell ; and the rife in lands is a misfortune to the poor, where their wages do

do not rife proportionably, which will not
happen where manufactures and agriculture
are not fufficiently encouraged. Give premiums by land or by water, arrange your
exports and imports in what manner you
will; if you difcourage the people from
working up the principal materials of their
country, the bulk of that people muft ever
continue miferable, the growth of the nation
will be checked, and the finews of the ftate
enfeebled.

I have ftated a tedious detail of inftances,
to fhew that the fufferings of the lower
claffes of our people have continued the
fame (with an exception only of thofe employed in the linen trade) fince the time of
queen Anne, as they were during her reign ;
that the caufe remains the fame, namely,
that our manufacturers have not fufficient
employment, and fcannot afford to buy from
the farmer, and that therefore manufactures and agriculture muft both be prejudi-
ced.

After

After revolving thofe repeated inftances, and almoft continued chain of diftrefs, for fuch a feries of years, among the inhabitants of a temperate climate, furrounded by the bounties of providence and the means of abundance, and being unable to difcover any accidental or natural caufes for thofe evils, we are led to inquire whether they have arifen from the miftaken policy of man.

I have the honour to be,

My lord, &c.

G   T H E

THE

COMMERCIAL RESTRAINTS

OF

IRELAND

CONSIDERED.

FIFTH LETTER.

G 2

THE

COMMERCIAL RESTRAINTS

OF

IRELAND

CONSIDERED.

FIFTH LETTER.

My Lord,

Dublin, 30th Aug. 1779.

EVERY man of difcernment, who at-
tends to the facts which have been ftated,
would conclude, that there muft be fome
political inftitutions in this country counteracting the natural courfe of things, and
obftructing the profperity of the people.
Thofe inftitutions fhould be confidered,
that as from the effects the caufe has been
traced, this alfo fhould be examined, to
fhew that fuch confequences are neceffarily deducible from it. For feveral years
the

the exportation of live cattle to England*
was the principal trade of Ireland. This
was thought moſt erroneouſly, ‡ as has ſince
been acknowledged §, to lower the rents of
lands in England. From this and perhaps
from ſome leſs worthy motive ** a law paſſed
in England ††, to reſtrain and afterwards
to prohibit the exportation of cattle from
Ireland. The Iriſh deprived of their principal trade, and reduced to the utmoſt diſtreſs by this prohibition, had no reſource but
to work up their own commodities, to which
they applied themſelves with great ardor ‡‡.
After this prohibition they increaſed their
number of ſheep, and at the revolution were
poſſeſſed of very numerous flocks. They had

good

* Carte, 2 vol. 318, 319.

‡ Sir W. Petty's Political Survey, 69, 70.   Sir W.
Temple, 3 vol. 22, 23.

§ By ſeveral Britiſh acts (32 G. 2, ch. 11. 5 G. 3,
ch. 10. 12 G. 3, ch. 56.) allowing from time to time the
free importation of all ſorts of cattle from Ireland.

** Perſonal prejudice againſt the duke of Ormond. (2
Carte, 332, 337.

†† 15 Ch. 2, ch. 7. 18 Ch. 2, ch. 2.

‡‡ 2 Carte, 332.

good reafons to think that this objeƐ of induftry was not only left open, but recommended to them. The ineffeƐual attempt by
lord Strafford in 1639, to prevent the making
of broad cloths in Ireland *, the relinquifh-
ment of that fcheme by never afterwards
reviving it, the encouragement given to
their woollen manufaƐures by many Englifh aƐs of parliament from the reign of
Edward the 3d † to the 12th of Ch. 2d, and
feveral of them for the exprefs purpofe of
exportation ; the letter of Charles the 2d,
in 1667, with the advice of his privy council in England, and the proclamation in
purfuance of that letter, encouraging the
exportation of their manufaƐures to foreign
countries ; by the Irifh ftatutes of the 12th
Hen. 8, ch. 2, 28th Hen. 8, ch. 17, of the 11th
Elizabeth, Ch. 10, and 17 and 18 Ch. 2,
ch. 15, (all of which, the aƐ of 28 Henry 8th
excepted, received the approbation of the
privy council of England, having been returned

* Com. Jour. 1 vol. p. 208, by a claufe to be infert-
ed in an Irifh aƐ.

† See poft, thofe aƐs ftated.

turned under the great feal of that kingdom) afforded as ftrong grounds of affurance as any country could poffefs for the continuance of any trade or manufacture.

Great numbers of their flocks had been deftroyed at the time of the revolution, but they were replaced at great expence, and became more numerous and flourifhing than before. The woollen manufacture was cultivated in Ireland for ages before, and for feveral years after the revolution, without any appearance of jealoufy from England, the attempt by lord Strafford excepted. No difcouragement is intimated in any fpeech from the throne until the year 1698, lord Sydney's in 1692 imparts the contrary, " their " majefties, fays he*, being in their own roy- " al judgments fatisfied that a country fo " fertile by nature, and fo advantageoufly " fituated for *trade and navigation*, can want " nothing but the bleffing of peace, and the " help of fome good laws to make it as rich " and flourifhing *as moft of its neighbours*; I am " ordered to affure you, that nothing fhall " be

Com. Jour 2 Vol. p. 576.

" be wanting on their parts that may con-
" tribute to your perfect and lasting hap-
" pinefs."

Several laws had been made * in England
to prevent the exportation of wool, yarn
made of wool, fuller's earth, or any kind of
fcowering earth or fulling clay from England
or Ireland, into any places out of the kingdoms of England or Ireland.   But thofe
laws were equally reftrictive on both kingdoms.

In the firft year‡ of William and Mary
certain ports were mentioned in Ireland, from
which only wool fhould be fhipped from that
kingdom, and certain ports in England into
which only it fhould be imported; and a re-
gifter was directed to be kept in the cuftom-
houfe of London of all the wool, from time
to time, imported from Ireland.   By a fubfequent act in this reign†, paffed in 1696,
the commiffioners or farmers of the cuftoms
in

* Englifh acts, 12 Ch. 2 ch. 32. 13 and 14 Ch. 2 ch. 18.
‡ 1 W. and M. Ch. 32.   † 7 and 8 W. ch. 28.

in Ireland are directed, once in every fix months, to tranfmit to the commiffioners of cuftoms in England, an account of all wool exported from Ireland to England, and this laft act, in its title, profeffes the intention of encouraging the importation of wool from Ireland. The prohibition of exporting the materials from either kingdom, except to the other, and the encouragement to export it from Ireland to England, mentioned in the title of the laft-mentioned act, but for which no provifion feems to be made, unlefs the defignation of particular ports may be fo called, was the fyftem that then feemed to be fettled, for preventing the wool of Ireland from being prejudicial to England; but the prevention of the exportation of the manufacture was an idea that feemed never to have been entertained until the year 1697, when a bill for that purpofe was brought into the Englifh houfe of commons*, and paffed that houfe; but after great confideration was not paffed by the lords in that parliament.

14th Jan. 1697.

parliament †. There does not appear to have been any increafe at that time in the woollen manufacture of Ireland, fufficient to have raifed any jealoufy in England.

By a report from the commiffioners of trade in that kingdom, dated on the 23d December 97, and laid before the houfe of commons, in 1698 they find that the woollen manufacture in Ireland had increafed fince the year 1665, as follows :

Years.	New draperies Pieces.	Old draperies. Pieces.	Frize Yards.
1665	224	32	444,381
1687	11,360	103	1,129,716
1696	4,413	34½	104,167

The bill for reftraining the exportation of woollen manufactures from Ireland was brought into the Englifh houfe of commons on the 23d of Feb. 97, but the law did not pafs until the year 1699, in the firft feffion of the new parliament. I have not been

able

† 7 July 1698 diffolved

able to obtain an account of the exportation of woollen manufactures for the year 1697 †, but from the 25th of December 1697, to the 25th of December 1698, being the first year in which the exports in books extant, are regiftered in the cuftom-houfe at Dublin, the amount appears to be of

New drapery. Pieces.	Old drapery. Pieces.	Frize. Yds.
23,285$\frac{1}{2}$	281$\frac{1}{2}$	666,901

though this encreafe of export fhews that the trade was advancing in Ireland, yet the total amount or the comparative increafe fince

† In a pamphlet cited by Dr. Smith, (v. 2, p. 244.) in his memoirs, of wool it is faid that the total value of thofe manufactures exported in 1697, was 23,614l 9s 6d namely, in frizes and ftockings 14,625l 12s ; in old and new draperies 8988l 17s 6d, and that though the Irifh had been every year increafing yet they had not recovered a-bove one third of the woollen trade which they had be-fore the war (ib. 243). The value in 1687, according to the fame authority, was 70,521l 14s, of which the frizes were 56,485l 16s. Stockings 2520l. 18s, and old and new drapery (which it is there faid could alone interfere with the Englifh trade) 11,514l 10s.

fince 1687 could fcarcely " fink the value of
" lands, and tend to the ruin of the trade
" and woollen manufactures of England §."

The apprehenfions of England feem rather to have arifen from the fears of future,
than from the experience of any paft rivalfhip in this trade. I have more than once
heard lord Bowes, the late chancellor of this
kingdom, mention a converfation that he
had with fir Robert Walpole on this fubject,
who affured him that the jealoufies entertained in England, of the woollen trade in
Ireland, and the reftraints of that trade had
at firft taken their rife from the boafts of
fome of our countrymen in London, of the
great fuccefs of that manufacture here.
Whatever was the caufe, both houfes of parliament in England addreffed king William,
in very ftrong terms, on this fubject; but
on confidering thofe addreffes they feem to
be founded, not on the ftate at that time of
that manufacture here, but the probability
of

§ Preamble of Englifh act of 1699.

of its further increase. As those proceedings
are of great importance to two of the principal manufactures of this country, it is
thought necessary to state them particularly.
The lords represent, " that the *growing* ma-
" nufacture of cloth in Ireland ‡, both by the
" cheapness of all forts of necessaries for
" life, and *goodness of materials for making all*
" *manner of cloth*, doth invite your subjects
" of England with their families and fer-
" vants to leave their habitations to settle
" there, to the increase of the woollen ma-
" nufacture in Ireland, which makes your
" loyal subjects in this kingdom very appre-
" henfive that *the further growth* of it *may*
" greatly prejudice the said manufacture
" here; by which the trade of the nation
" and the value of lands will very much de-
" creafe, and the numbers of your people be
" much leffened here;" they then befeech
his majefty " in the moft public and effec-
" tual way, that may be, to declare to all
" your fubjects of Ireland, that the *growth*
                                    " and

‡ 9th June 1698, vol. of lords journals, page 314.

" and *increafe* of the woollen manufacture
" hath long, and will ever be looked upon
" with jealoufy, by all your fubjects of this
" kingdom; *and if not timely remedied* may
" occafion very ftrict laws, totally to prohi-
" bit and fupprefs the fame; and on the
" other hand if they turn their induftry and
" fkill, to the fettling and improving the
" linen manufacture, for which generally
" the lands of that kingdom are very pro-
" per, they fhall receive all countenance, fa-
" vour and protection from your *royal influ-*
" *ence*, for the encouragement and promo-
" ting of the faid linen manufacture, to *all*
" *the advantage and profit that kingdom can be*
" *capable of.*"

King William in his anfwer fays, "his
majefty will take care to do what their lord-
fhips have defired;" and the lords direct that
the lord chancellor fhould order that the
addrefs and anfwer be forthwith printed
and publifhed §.

In

§ Lord's Jour. page 315.'

In the addrefs of the commons § they fay,
that " being fenfible that the wealth and
" peace of this kingdom do, in a great mea-
" fure, depend on preferving the woollen
" manufacture, as much as poffible, *entire*
" to this realm, they think it becomes them,
" like their anceftors, to be jealous of the
" *eftablifhment* and *increafe* thereof elfewhere;
" and to ufe their utmoft endeavours to pre-
" vent it, and therefore, they cannot with-
" out trouble obferve, that Ireland, depen-
" dant on, and protected by England in the
" enjoyment of all they have, and which is
" fo proper for the linen manufacture, the
" eftablifhment and growth of which there
" would be fo enriching to themfelves, and
" fo profitable to England, fhould *of late*
" apply itfelf to the woollen manufacture,
" to the great prejudice of the trade of this
" kingdom, and fo unwillingly promote the
" linen trade, which would benefit both
" them and us.

The

§ 30th June 1698.

" The confequence whereof will neceffitate
" your parliament of England to interpofe, to
" prevent the mifchief that *threatens* us, un-
" lefs your majefty, by your authority and
" great wifdom, fhall find means to fecure
" the trade of England by making your fub-
" jects of Ireland to purfue the joint inte-
" reft of both kingdoms."

" And we do moft humbly implore your
" majefty's protection and favour in this
" matter; and that you will make it your
" royal care, and enjoin all thofe you em-
" ploy in Ireland, to make it their care, and
" ufe their utmoft diligence, to hinder the
" *exportation of wool* from Ireland, except to
" be imported hither, and for the difcourag-
" ing the woollen manufactures, and encou-
" raging the linen manufactures in Ireland,
" to which we fhall be *always* ready to give
" our *utmoft* affiftance."

This addrefs was prefented to his majefty
by the houfe. The anfwer is explicit. " I
" fhall do all that in me lies to difcourage

H   " the

" the woollen trade in Ireland, and encou-
" rage the linen manufacture there; and
" to promote the trade of England."

He foon after wrote a letter § to lord Gal-
way, then one of the lords juftices of this
kingdom, in which he tells him, "that it
" was never of fuch importance to have at
" prefent a good feffion of parliament, not
" only in regard to my affairs of that king-
" dom, but efpecially of this here. The chief
" thing that muft be tried to be prevented is,
" that the Irifh parliament takes no notice of
" what has paffed in this here†, and that you
" make effectual laws for the linen manufac-
" ture, and difcourage *as far as poffible* the
" woollen." It would be unjuft to infer
from any of thofe proceedings that this
great prince wanted affection for this country. They were times of party. He was
often under the neceffity of complying a-
gainft his own opinion and wifhes, and a-
bout this time was obliged to fend away his
favourite

§ 16th July 1698.   † Rapin's Hift. v. 17, p. 417.

favourite guards, in compliance with the defire of the commons.

The houfes of parliament in England o-
riginally intended, that the bufinefs fhould
be done in the parliament of Ireland by the
exertion of that great and juft influence
which king William had acquired in that
kingdom. On the firft day of the following
feffion § the lords juftices, in their fpeech,
mention a bill tranfmitted for the encouragement of the linen and hempen manufactures, which they recommend in the
following words, " the fettlement of this
" manufacture will contribute much to peo-
" ple the country, and will be found *much*
" *more advantageous to this kingd m* than the
" woollen manufacture, which being the
" fettled ftaple trade of England, *from*
" *whence all foreign markets* are fupplied, can
" never be encouraged *here* for that purpofe;
" whereas the linen and hempen manufac-
" tures will not only be encouraged, as con-
H 2   " fiftent

§ 27th September 1698, vol. 2. p. 994.

" fiftent with the trade of England, but will
" render the trade of this kingdom both ufe-
" ful and neceffary to England."

The commons in their addrefs § promife
their hearty endeavours to eftablifh a linen
and hempen manufacture in Ireland, and fay
that they hoped to find fuch a temperament
in refpect to the woollen trade here, that
the fame may not be injurious to England.
They referred the confideration of that fubject to the committee of fupply, who 'refolved that an additional duty be laid on old
and new drapery of the manufacture of this
kingdom † that fhall be exported, frizes excepted ; to which the houfe agreed *. But
there were petitions prefented againft this
duty, and relative to the quantity of it, and
the committee appointed to confider of this
duty were not it feems fo expeditious in
their proceedings as the impatience of the
times required ‡.

On

§ Com. Jour. 2 Vol. p. 997. † Ib. 2 vol. p. 1022.
* October 24, 1698.
‡ Com. Jour. v. 2, p. 1007, 1035.

On the 2d of October the lords juftices made a quickening fpeech to both houfes, taking notice, that the progrefs which they expected was not made, in the bufinefs of the feffion, and ufe thofe remarkable words, " The matters we recommended to you are fo " neceffary, and the profperity of this king- " dom depends fo much on the good fuccefs " of this feffion, that fince we know his " majefty's affairs cannot permit your fitting " very long, we thought the greateft mark " we could give of our kindnefs and con- " cern for you, was to come hither, and " defire you to haften the difpatch of the " matters under your confideration; in " which we are the more carneft, becaufe " we muft be fenfible, that if the prefent " opportunity his majefty's affection to you " hath put into your hands be loft, it feems " hardly to be recovered t."

On the 2d of January 1698, O. S. the houfe refolved, that the report from the committee of the whole houfe, appointed to confider

---

† Com. Jour. p. 1032.

confider of a duty to be laid on the woollen manufactures of this kingdom, should be made on the next day, and nothing to intervene. But on that day a meffage was delivered from the lords juftices in the following words, " We have received his ma- " jeftys commands † to fend unto you a bill, " entitled an act for laying an additional " duty upon woollen manufactures exported " out of this kingdom; the paffing of which " in this feffion his majefty recommends to " you, as what may be of great advantage " for the prefervation of the trade of this " kingdom."

The bill which accompanied this meffage was prefented, and a queftion for receiving it was carried in the affirmative, by 74 a- gainft 34. This bill muft have been tranfmit- ed from the council of Ireland. Whilft the commons were proceeding with the utmoft temper and moderation, were exerting great firmnefs in reftraining all attempts to enflame

the

† Com. Jour. 2 Vol. p. 1082.

the minds of the people†, and were deliberating on the moſt important ſubject that
could ariſe, it was taken out of their hands‡;
but the bill paſſed though not without op-
poſition *, and received the royal aſſent on
the 29th day of January 1698.

By this act an additional duty was im-
poſed of 4s. for every 20s. in value of broad
cloth exported out of Ireland, and 2s. on e-
very 20s. in value of new drapery, frizes
only excepted, from the 25th of March 99,
to the 25th March, 1702 ‖; the only woollen
manufacture excepted was one of which Ireland had been in poſſeſſion before the reign
of Edward the 3d, and in which ſhe had
been always diſtinguiſhed ‡. This law has
every appearance of having being framed
on the part of adminiſtration.

But

Com. Jour. 2 vol. 1007.   * Com. Jour. 1104, by
105, againſt 41.   ‖ 10 W. 3 ch. 5.

‡ And. on Com. Vol. 1. 204.

§ The commiſſioners of trade in England by their re-
preſentation of the 11th October 1698, ſay, (Eng. Com.
Jour. 12 vol. 437.) "they conceive it not neceſſary to
make any alteration whatſoever in this act," but take
notice that the duties on broad cloth, of which very little is
made in Ireland, is 20 per cent; but the duty on new drapery, of which much is made, is but 10 per cent.

but it did not fatisfy the Englifh parliament, where a perpetual law was made, prohibiting, from the 20th of June, 1699*, the exportation from Ireland of all goods made or mixed with wool, except to England and Wales, and with the licenfe of the commiffioners of the revenue; duties+ had been before laid on the importation into England equal to a prohibition, therefore this act has operated as a total prohibition of the exportation.

Before thefe laws the Irifh were under great difadvantages in the woollen trade, by not being allowed to export their woollen manufactures to the Englifh colonies§, or to import dye ftuffs directly from thence; and the Englifh in this refpect, and in havin thofe exclufive markets, poffeffed confiderable advantages.

Let it now be confidered what are the ufual means taken to promote the profperity

* Eng. Stat. 10 and 11 Wil. III. ch. 10, paffed in 1699.   † 12 Ch. II. ch. 4, Eng. and afterward's continued by 11 Geo. I. ch. 7. Brit.

§ By an Eng, act, made in 1663, the fame which laid the firft reftraint on the exportation of cattle.

rity of any country in refpect of trade and
manufactures. She is encouraged to work
up her own materials, to export her manufactures to other nations, to import from
them the materials for manufacture, and
to export none of her own that fhe is able
to work up, not to buy what fhe is capable of felling to others, and to promote the
carrying trade and fhip-building. If thefe
are the moft obvious means by which a
nation may advance in ftrength and riches,
inftitutions counteracting thofe means muft
neceffarily tend to reduce it to weaknefs
and poverty; and therefore the advocates
for the continuance of thofe inftitutions
will find it difficult to fatisfy the world that
fuch a fyftem of policy is either reafonable
or juft.

The cheapnefs of labour, the excellence
of materials, and the fuccefs of the manufacture in the excluded country *, may appear to an unprejudiced man to be rather rea-

fons

* See the Addrefs of the Englifh Houfe of Lords.

fons for the encouragement than for the
prohibition. But the preamble of the
Englifh act of the 10th and 11th of William
III. affirms, that the exportation from Ireland and the Englifh plantations in America to foreign markets, heretofore fupplied
from England, would inevitably fink the
value of lands, and tend to the ruin of the
trade and manufactures of that realm. I
fhall only confider this affertion as relative
to Ireland. A fact upon which the happinefs of a great and ancient kingdom, and
of millions of people depends, ought to
have been fupported by the moft incontefti-
ble evidence, and fhould never be fuffered
to reft in fpeculation, or to be taken from
the mere fuggeftion or diftant apprehenfion
of commercial jealoufy. Thofe fears for
the future were not founded on any experience of the paft. From what market had
the woollen manufactures of Ireland ever
excluded England? What part of her trade,
and which of her manufactures had been
ruined, and where did any of her lands fall
by the woollen exports of Ireland? Were
any

any of thofe facts attempted to be proved at
the time of the prohibition? The amount
of the Irifh export proves it to have been
impoffible that thofe facts could have then
exifted. The confequences mentioned as
likely to arife to England from the fuppofed
increafe of thofe manufactures in Ireland,
had no other foundation but the apprehenfions of rivalfhip among trading people,
who, in excluding their fellow-citizens,
have opened the gates for the admiffion of
the enemy.

Whether thofe apprehenfions are now
well founded, fhould be carefully confidered. Juftice, found policy, and the general
good of the Britifh empire require it. The
arguments in fupport of thofe reftraints are
principally thefe:—That labour is cheaper
and taxes lower in Ireland than in England,
and that the former would be able to under fell the latter in all foreign markets.

Spinning is now certainly cheaper in Ireland, becaufe the perfons employed in it
live

live on food* with which the Englifh would
not be content; but the wages of fpinners
would foon rife if the trade was opened.
At the loom, I am informed, that the fame
quantity of work is done cheaper in England than in Ireland; and we have the misfortune of daily experience to convince us
that the Englifh, notwithftanding the fuppofed advantages of the Irifh in this trade,
underfell them at their own markets in every branch of the woollen manufacture. A
decifive proof that they cannot underfell
the Englifh in foreign markets.

With the increafe of manufactures, agriculture and commerce in Ireland, the demand for labour, and confequently its price,
would increafe §. That price would be foon
higher in Ireland than in England. It is not
in the richeft countries, but in thofe that
are growing rich the fafteft, that the wages
of labour are higheft †, though the price
of

---

* Potatoes and milk, or more frequently water.
§ Dr. Smith's Wealth of Nations, 1 vol. p. 94.
† Ib. 85, 86.

of provifions is much lower in the latter; this, before the prefent rebellion, was in both refpects the cafe of England and North America.   Any difference in the price of labour is more than balanced by the difference in the price of the material, which has been for many years paft higher in Ireland than in England, and would become more valuable if the export of the mannfacture was allowed.   The Englifh have alfo great advantages in this trade from their habits of diligence, fuperior fkill and large capitals. From thefe circumftances, though the Scotch have full liberty to export their woollen manufactures, the Englifh work up their wool*, and the Scotch make only fome kinds of coarfe cloaths for the lower claffes of their people; and this is faid to be for want of a capital to manufacture it at home §.   If the woollen trade was now open to Ireland, it would be for the moft part

* Dr. Smith's Wealth of Nations, 1 Vol. p. 445. Dr. Campbell's Polit. Survey of Great Britain, 2 Vol. p. 159.   Anderfon on Induftry.

§ Smith, ib.

part carried on by Englifh capitals, and by
merchants refident there. Nearly one half
of the ftock which carried on the foreign
trade of Ireland in 1672, inconfiderable as
it then was, belonged to thofe who lived
out of Ireland *. The greater part of the
exportation and coafting trade of Britifh
America was carried on by the capitals of
merchants who refided in Great Britain;
even many of the ftores and ware-houfes
from which goods were retailed in fome of
their principal provinces, particularly in Vir-
ginia and Maryland, belonged to merchants
who refided in Great Britain, and the retail
trade was carried on by thofe who were not
refident in the country †. It is faid that in
ancient Egypt, China and Indoftan, the
greater part of their exportation trade was
carried on by foreigners §. The fame thing
happened formerly in Ireland, where the
whole commerce of the country was carried
on by the Dutch ‡; and at prefent in the
victualling

* Sir Wil. Petty's Polit. Survey of Ireland, p. 90.
† Smith's Wealth of Nations, 1 Vol. p. 446.   § Ib.
‡ Lord Strafford's Letters, 1 Vol. p. 33.

victualling trade of Ireland, the Irifh are but factors to the Englifh. This is not without example in Great Britain, where there are many little manufacturing towns, the inhabitants of which have not capitals fufficient to tranfport the produce of their own induftry to thofe diftant markets where there is demand and confumption for it, and their merchants are properly only the agents of wealthier merchants, who refide in fome of the greater commercial cities †. The Irifh are deficient in all kinds of ftock, they have not fufficient for the cultivation of their lands, and are deficient in the ftocks of mafter manufacturers, wholefale merchants, and even of retailers.

Of what Ireland gains it is computed that one third centers in Great Britain §. Of our woollen manufacture the greateft part of the profit would go directly there. But the manufacturers of Ireland would be employed, would

† Smith's Wealth of Nations, 1 Vol. p. 445.
§ Sir M. Decker's decline of foreign trade, p. 155, and Anderfon on Commerce, 2 Vol. p. 149.

would be enabled to buy from the farmers the fuperfluous produce of their labour, the people would become induftrious, their numbers would greatly increafe, the Britifh ftate would be ftrengthened, though probably this country would not for many years find any great influx of wealth ; it would be however more equally diftributed, from which the people and the government would derive many important advantages.

Whatever wealth might be gained by Ireland would be, in every refpeĉt, an acceffion to Great Britain. Not only a confiderable part of it would flow to the feat of government, and of final judicature, and to the centre of commerce ; but when Ireland fhould be able fhe would be found willing, as in juftice fhe ought to be, to bear her part of thofe expences which Great Britain may hereafter incur, in her efforts for the protecti-on of the whole Britifh empire. If Ireland chearfully and fpontaneoufly, but when fhe was ill able, contributed, particularly in the years 1759, 1761 and 1769, and continued

to

to do fo in the midft of diftrefs and poverty, without murmur, to the end of the year 1778, when Great Britain thought proper to relieve her from a burden which fhe was no longer able to bear, no doubt can be entertained of her contributing, in a much greater proportion, when the means of acquiring fhall be opened to her.

I form this opinion, not only from the proofs which the experience of many years, and in many fignal inftances has given, but the nature of the Irifh conftitution, which requires that the laws of Ireland fhould be certified under the great feal of England, and the fuperintending protection of Great Britain, neceffary to the exiftence of Ireland, would make it her intereft to cultivate, at all times, a good underftanding with her fifter kingdom.

The lownefs of taxes in Ireland feems to fall within the objection arifing from the cheapnefs of labour. But the difproportion between the taxes of the two kingdoms is much overrated in Great Britain. Hearth-money

I   in

in Ireland amounts to about 59,000l. yearly, the fums raifed by Grand Juries are faid to exceed the annual fum of 140,000l. and the duties on beef, butter, pork and tallow exported, at a medium from 1772 to 1778, amount to 26,577l. 11s. yearly. Thefe are payable out of lands, or their immediate produce, and may well be confidered as a land tax. Thefe with the many other taxes payable in Ireland, compared either with the annual amount of the fums which the inhabitants can earn or expend, with the rentall of the lands, the amount of the circulating fpecie, of perfonal property, or of the trade of Ireland, it is apprehended would appear not to be inferior in proportion to the taxes of England, compared with any of thofe objects in that country†. The fums remitted to abfentees *, are worfe than fo much

---

† Compare the circumftances of the two countries in one of thofe articles, which affects all the reft. The fums raifed in Great Britain in time of peace are faid to amount to ten millions, in Ireland to more than one million yearly. The circulating cafh of the former is eftimated at 23 millions, of the latter at two.

See poft. 59.

much paid in taxes, becaufe a large proportion of thefe is ufually expended in the
country. If this reafoning is admitted, it
will require no calculation to fhew that
Ireland pays more taxes in proportion to its
fmall income, than England does in proportion to its great one.

Of excifable commodities, the confumption by each manufacturer is not fo confiderable as to make the great difference
commonly imagined in the price of labour.
It is an acknowledged fact that Ireland
pays in excifes as much as fhe is able to
bear, and that her inability to bear more
arifes from thofe very reftraints. But fuppofing the difproportion to be as great as is
erroneoufly imagined in Great Britain, it
will not conclude in favour of the prohibition. The land-tax is nearly four times as
high in fome counties of England as in
others, and provifions are much cheaper in
fome parts of that kingdom than in others,
and yet they have all fufficient employment,
and go to market upon equal terms. But a

I 2   monopoly

monopoly and not an equal market was plainly the object in 1698 ; it was not to prevent the Irish from underfelling at foreign markets, but to prevent their felling there at all. The confequences to the excluded country have been mentioned. England has alfo been a great fufferer by this miftaken policy.

Mr. Dobbs, who wrote in 1729 *, affirms that by this law of 1699, our woollen manufacturers were forced away into France, Germany and Spain ; that they had in many branches fo much improved the woollen manufacture of France, as not only to fupply themfelves, but to vie with the English in foreign markets, and that by their correfpondence, they had laid the foundation for the running of wool thither both from England and Ireland. He fays that thofe nations were then fo improved, as in a great meafure to fupply themfelves with many forts they formerly had from England, and fince that time have deprived

Britain

* Effay on the Trade of Ireland, p. 6, 7.

Britain of millions, inftead of the thoufands that Ireland might have made.

It is now acknowledged that the French
underfell the Englifh; and as far as they
are fupplied with Irifh wool, the lofs to the
Britifh empire is double what it would be,
if the Irifh exported their goods manufactured. This is mentioned by Sir Matthew
Decker *, as the caufe of the decline of
the Englifh, and the increafe of the
French woollen manufactures; and he
afferts that the Irifh can recover that
trade out of their hands. England, fince
the paffing this law, has got much lefs
of our wool than before †. In 1698, the
export of our wool to England amounted to
377,520¾ ftone; at a medium of eight years,
to lady-day 1728, it was only 227,049 ftone,
which is 148,000 ftone lefs than in 1698,
and was a lofs of more than half a million
yearly to England. In the laft ten years
the quantity exported has been fo greatly
reduced, that in one of thefe years ‡ it a-
                            ·   mounted

* Decline of foreign trade, p. 55, 56, 155.
† Dobbs, p. 76.   ‡ In 1774.

mounted only to 1007ft. 11lb. and in the laft year did not exceed 1665 ft. 12lb. *. The price of wool, under an abfolute prohibition, is 5ol. or 6ol. per cent. under the market price of Europe, which will always defeat the prohibition †.

The impracticability of preventing the pernicious practice of running wool is now well underftood. Of the thirty-two counties in Ireland nineteen are maritime, and the reft are wafhed by a number of fine rivers that empty themfelves into the fea. Can fuch an extent of ocean, fuch a range of coafts, fuch a multitude of harbours, bays and creeks be effectually guarded?

The prohibition of the export of live cattle forced the Irifh into the re-eftablifhment

* Nor was this deficiency made up by the exportation of yarn. The quantities of thefe feveral articles exported from 1764 to 1778, are mentioned in the Appendix, Numb.

† Smith's Memoirs of Wool, 2 Vol. p. 554. The only way to prevent it, is to enable us to work it up at home, Ib. 293.

ment of their woollen manufacture; and the reftraint of the woollen manufacture was a ftrong temptation to the running of wool. The fevereft penalties were enacted, the Britifh legiflature, the government and houfe of commons of Ireland, exerted all poffible efforts to remove this growing evil, but in vain, until the law was made in Great Britain * in 1739, to take off the duties from woollen or bay yarn exported from Ireland, excepting worfted yarn of two or more threads, which has certainly given a confiderable check to the running of wool, and has fhewn that the policy of opening is far more efficacious than that of reftraining. The world is become a great commercial fociety, exclude trade from one channel, and it feldom fails to find another.

To fhew the abfolute neceffity of Great Britain's opening to Ireland fome new means of acquiring, let the annual balance of exports and

* This was done for the benefit of the woollen manufacture in England. Eng. Com. Jour. 22 Vol. p. 414.

and imports, returned from the entries in
the different cuſtom houſes, in favour of
Ireland, on all her trade with the whole
world, in every year from 1768 to 1778,
be compared with the remittances made
from Ireland to England in each of thoſe
years, it will evidently appear that thoſe
remittances could not be made out of that
balance. The entries of exports made at
cuſtom houſes are well known to exceed
the real amount of thoſe exports in all
countries, and this exceſs is greater in times
of diffidence, when merchants wiſh to acquire credit by giving themſelves the appearance of being great traders.

This balance in favour of 'Ireland on
her general trade, appears by thoſe returns
to have been in 1776, 606,190l. 11s. 0½d.
in 1777, 24,203l. 3s. 10½d. in 1778,
386,384l. 5s. 7d. and taken at a medium
of eleven years from 1768 to 1778, both
incluſive, it amounts to the ſum of
605,083l. 7s. 5d. The ſums remitted from
Ireland to Great-Britain for rents, intereſt
of

of money, penfions, falaries and profits of
offices amounted, at the loweft computation,
from 1768 to 1773, to 1,100,000l. yearly * ;
and from 1773, when the tontines were introduced, from which period large fums
were borrowed from England, thofe remittances were confiderably increafed, and
are now not lefs than between 12 and 13000l.
yearly. Ireland then pays to Great-Britain
double the fum that fhe collects from the
whole world in all the trade which Great-
Britain allows her. It will be difficult to
find a fimilar inftance in the hiftory of man-
kind.

Thofe great and conftant iffues of her
wealth without any return, not felt by
any other country in fuch a degree, are
reafons for granting advantages to Ireland
to fupply this confuming wafte, inftead of
depriving her of any which Nature has beftowed.

* This is ftated confiderably under the computation
made in the lift of abfentees publifhed in Dublin in 1769,
which makes the amount at that time 1,208,982l. 14s. 6d.

If any of the refources, which have hitherto enabled her to bear this prodigious drain, are injurious to the manufactures both of England and Ireland, and highly advantageous to the rivals and enemies of both, is it wife in Great-Britain by perfevering in an impracticable fyftem of commercial policy, repugnant to the natural courfe and order of things, to fuffer fo very confiderable a part of the empire to remain in fuch a fituation?

The experiment of an equal and reafonable fyftem of commerce is worth making; that which has been found the beft conductor in philofophy is the fureft guide in commerce.

Would you confult perfons employed in the trade? They have in one refpect an intereft oppofite to that of the public. To narrow the competition is advantageous to the dealers *, but prejudicial to the public. If Edward the firft had not preferred the general

* Smith's Wealth of Nations, 1 Vol. 316.

general welfare of his fubjects to the interefted opinions and petitions of the traders,
all merchant traders (who were then moft-
ly ftrangers) would have been fent away
from London †, for which purpofe the commons offered him the 50th part of their
moveables*.

What was the information given by the
trading towns in 1697 and 1698, on the
fubject of the woollen manufacture of Ireland, feveral of their §-petitions ftate that
the woollen manufacture was *fet up* in Ireland, as if it had been lately introduced
there; and one of them goes fo far as to
reprefent the [particular time and manner
of introducing it. " Many 'of the poor of
" that kingdom, fays this extraordinary
" petition, during the late rebellion there,
" fled into the Weft of England, where
" they were put to work in the woolen
manu-

† Anderfon on Com. 1 Vol. 131.

* The wifh of traders for a monopoly is not confined
to England ; in the fame kingdom fome parts are reftrained
in favour of others, as in Sweden to this hour. Abbe
Refnal 2 Vol. 28.

§ Eng. Com. Journ. 12 Vol. 64, 68.

‡ Eng. Com. Jonrn. 12 Vol. 64.

" manufacture to learn that trade, and fince
" the reduction of Ireland *endeavours were*
" *ufed* to *fet up* thofe manufactures there."

Would any man fuppofe that this could
relate to a manufacture, in which this kingdom excelled before the time of Edward the
3d, which had been the fubject of fo many
laws in both kingdoms, and which was always cultivated here, and before this rebellion with more fuccefs than after it? the
trading towns gave accounts totally inconfiftent of the ftate of this manufacture at
that time in England: from Exeter it is reprefented as greatly decayed and difcouraged *
in thofe parts; and diminifhed in England.
But a petition from Leeds reprefents this
manufacture as having very much increafed†
fince the revolution in all its feveral branches, to the general intereft of England; and
yet, in two days after the clothiers from
three towns in Gloucefterfhire affert, that
the trade has decayed, and that the poor are
almoft ftarved‡. The commiffioners of
trade differ in opinion from them, and by
their

* Englifh Com. Journ. vol. 12, p. 7.
† Ib. 527.   ‡ Ib. 530.

their report, it appears that the woollen manufacture was then very much increafed and improved †. The traders have fometimes miftaken their own interefts on thofe fubjects; in 1698, a petition for prohibiting the importation from Ireland of all worfted and and woollen yarn, reprefents that the poor of England are ready to perifh by this importation *; and in 1739, feveral petitions were preferred againft taking off the duties § from worfted and bay yarn exported from Ireland to England. But this has been done in the manner before-mentioned, and is now acknowledged to be highly ufeful to England. Trading people have ever aimed at exclufive privileges; of this there are two extraordinary inftances; in the year 1698, two petitions were preferred, from Folkftone and Aldborough, ftating a fingular grievance that they fuffered from Ireland, " by the Irifh catching herrings *at Waterford* " *and Wexford* ‡ and fending them to the " Streights, and thereby *forefalling* and ruin- " ing petitioners markets;" but thefe petitioners

† Englifh Com. Jour. Vol. 12, p. 434.
* Ib. 387.　§ Ib. vol. 22.　‡ Ib. 178.

oners had the *hard lot* of having motions in their favour rejected.

I wifh that the fulleft information may be had in this important inveftigation, but between the inconfiftent accounts and opinions that will probably be given, experience only can decide ; and experience will demonftrate that the removal of thofe reftraints will promote the profperity of both kingdoms.

I have the honour to be,

My lord, &c.

T H E

THE

COMMERCIAL RESTRAINTS

OF

IRELAND

CONSIDERED.

SIXTH LETTER.

THE

COMMERCIAL RESTRAINTS

O F

IRELAND

C O N S I D E R E D.

S I X T H   L E T T E R.

My Lord,

Dublin, 1st September 1779.

BY the proceedings in the English parliament in the year 1698, and the speech of the
lords justices to the Irish parliament in that
year it appears, that the linen was intended to
be given to this country as an equivalent for
the woollen manufacture. The opinion that
this supposed equivalent was accepted of as
such by Ireland is mistaken. The temperament, which the commons of Ireland in their
addrefs said they hoped to find, was no more
than a partial and a temporary duty on the

K   exportation,

exportation, as an experiment only, and not as an eftablifhed fyftem, referving the exportation of frize, then much the moft valuable part to 'Ireland ‖. The Englifh intended the linen manufacture as a compenfation, and declared they thought it would be much more advantageous to Ireland * than the woollen trade.

This idea of an equivalent has led feveral perfons, and among the reft two very able writers †, into miftakes, from the want of information in fome facts which are neceffary to be known, that this tranfaction may be fully underftood, and therefore ought to be particularly ftated.

The

‡ The lords commiffioners of trade in England, by their report of the 31ft Auguft 1697, (Eng. Com. Jour. 12 vol. p. 428.) relating to the trade between England and Ireland, though they recommend the reftraining of the exportation of all forts of woollen manufactures out of Ireland, make the following exception, "except only, that of their " frize, as is wont, to England."

* See before Speech of lords Juftices.

† Mr. Dobbs, and after him Dr. Smith.

The Irifh had before this period applied themfelves to the linen trade. This appears by two of their ftatutes, in the reign of Elizabeth, one laying a duty on the export of flax and linen yarn ‡, and the other, making it felony to fhip them without paying fuch duty §. In the reign of Charles the 1ft, great pains were taken by lord Strafford to encourage this manufacture; and in the fucceeding reign + the great and munificent efforts of the firft duke of Ormond were crowned with merited fuccefs. The blafts of civil diffentions nipped thofe opening buds of induftry, and when the feafon was more favourable, it is probable that, like England, they found the woollen manufacture a more ufeful object of national purfuit; which may be collected from the addrefs of the Englifh houfe of commons, " that they fo unwillingly promote the linen " trade*;" and it was natural for a poor and

K 2 exhaufted

---

‡ 11 Elizabeth, feffion 3, ch. 10. § 13 Elizabeth, feffion 5, ch. 4. † 17 and 18 Ch. 2, ch. 9, for the advancement of the linen manufacture. Carte.

* See before.

exhaufted country to work up the materials of which it was poffeffed.

In 1696 the Englifh had given encourage-' ment to the manufactures of hemp and flax in Ireland, but without ftipulating any re- ftraint of the export of woollen goods. The Englifh act made in that year recites that great fums of money were yearly exported out of England, for the purchafing of hemp, flax and linen, and the productions thereof, which might be prevented by being fupplied from Ireland, and allows natives of England and Ireland to import into England free of all duties §, hemp and flax, and all the pro- ductions thereof.   In the fame feffion ‡ a law paffed in England for the more effectually preventing the exportation of wool, and for encouraging the importation thereof from Ireland. Both thofe manufactures were under the confideration of parliament this feffion, and it was thought, from enlarged views of the welfare of both kingdoms, that England fhould

§ 7 and 8 W. 3, ch. 39 from the 1ft of Auguft 1696.
   7 and 8 W. ch. 28.

ſhould encourage the linen, without diſcouraging the woollen manufacture of Ireland.
There was no further encouragement given
by England to our linen manufacture for
ſome years after the year 1696 *. *In* 1699,
there was no equivalent whatever given for the
prohibition of the export of our woollen
manufactures.

It is true, the aſſurances given by both
houſes of parliament in England, for the
encouragement of our linen trade, were as
ſtrong as words could expreſs; but was this
intended encouragement, if immediately
carried into execution, an equivalent to Ireland for what ſhe had loſt? let it firſt be
confidered whether it was an equivalent at
the time of the prohibition.

The woollen was then the principal
manufacture and trade of Ireland. That it
was then confidered as her ſtaple, appears
from the ſeveral acts of parliament before-
mentioned

* Not till the year 1705.

mentioned, and from the attempt made in 1695, by the Irifh houfe of commons, to lay a duty on all old and new drapery imported. The amount of the export proves§ the value of the trade to fo poor a country as Ireland, and makes it probable that fhe then clothed her own people. The addrefs of the Eng-lifh houfe of lords fhews that this manufac-ture was "growing" amongft us, and the goodnefs of our materials "for making *all manner* of cloth‡." And the Englifh act of 1698 is a voucher that this manufacture was then in fo flourifhing a ftate as to give apprehenfions, however ill-founded, of its rivalling England in foreign markets. The immediate confequences to Ireland fhewed the value of what fhe loft; many thoufand manufacturers were obliged to leave this kingdom for want of employment; many parts of the fouthern and weftern counties were fo far depopulated that they have not yet recovered a reafonable number of inha-bitants; and the whole kingdom was re-

duced

§ Com. Jour. 2 Vol. 725, 733. 16. vol. 360.
‡ See before.

duced to the greateſt poverty and diſtreſs *. The linen trade of Ireland was then of little conſideration, compared with the woollen †. ·The whole exportation of linens in 1700 ‡ amounted only in value to 14,i 12l. It was an experiment ſubſtituted in the place of an eſtabliſhed trade.

The Engliſh ports in Aſia, Africa and America were then ſhut againſt our linens, and when they were opened § for our white and brown linens, the reſtraints of imports from thence to Ireland made that conceſſion of leſs value, and ſhe ſtill found it her intereſt to ſend for the moſt part her linens to England, The linen could not have been a compenſation for the woollen manufacture which employs by far a greater number of hands, and yields much greater profit to the public, as well as to the manufacturers ‖. Of this manufacture there are not many countries which have the primum in equal perfection

* Dobbs 6, 7.   Com. Journ. 16 Vol. 362.
‡ Ib. 363.
§ By 3d and 4th Anne, ch. 9.
‖ And. on Comm. 2 Vol. 225. ·

perfection with England and Ireland, and no countries, taking in the various kinds of thofe extenfive manufactures, fo fit for carrying them on. There cannot be many rivals in this trade; in the linen they are moft numerous. Other parts of the world are more fit for it than Ireland, and many equally fo.

If this could be fuppofed to have been an equivalent at the time, or to have become fo by its fuccefs, it can no longer be confidered in that light. The commercial ftate of Europe is greatly altered. Ireland can no longer enjoy the benefit intended for her. It was intended that the great fums of money remitted out of England to foreign countries in this branch of commerce fhould all center in Ireland, and that England fhould be fupplied with linen from thence*; but foreigners now draw great fums from England in this trade, and rival

the

---

* This appears by the preamble to the Englifh act of the 7th and 8th W. III. c. 39.

the Irifh in the Englifh markets. The Ruffians are become powerful rivals to the Irifh and underfel them in the coarfe kinds of linen. This is now the ftaple manufacture of Scotland. England that had formerly cultivated this manufacture without fuccefs, and had taken linens * from France to the amount of 700,000l. yearly, has now made great progrefs in it. The encouragement of this trade in England and Scotland has been long a principal object to the Britifh legiflature, and the nation that encouraged us to the undertaking is now become our rival in it †; that this is not too ftrong an expreffion will appear by confidering two Britifh ftatutes, one of which ‡ has laid a duty on the importation of Irifh fail-cloth into Great-Britain, as long as the bounties fhould be paid on the exportation from § Ireland, which obliged us to

difcontinue

* Anderfon on Commerce, 2 Vol. 177.
† Com. Journ. 16 Vol. 365.
‡ In 1750.
§ By the law of 1750, and the bounties given on the
exportation

difcontinue them; and the other* has given a bounty on the exportation of *Britiſh* checquered and ſtripen linens exported out of *Great-Britain* to Africa, America, Spain, Portugal, Gibraltar, the iſland of Minorca, or the Eaſt-Indies. This is now become a very valuable part of the manufacture, which Great-Britain by the operation of this bounty keeps to herſelf. The bounties on the exportation of all other linen, which ſhe has generouſly given to ours as well as to her own † operate much more ſtrongly in favour of the latter‡; the expence of freight, inſurance, commiſſion, &c. in ſending

exportation of ſail-cloth from Great-Britain to foreign countries, Ireland has almoſt loſt this trade; ſhe cannot now ſupply herſelf. Great-Britain has not been the gainer; the quantities of ſail-cloth imported there in 1774, exceeding, according to the return from the cuſtom-houſe in London, the quantities imported in the year 1750, when the reſtrictive law was made. It has been taken from Ireland, and given to the Ruſſians, Germans, and Dutch. Ir. Com. Journ 16 Vol. 363.

* 10 G. III. ch.   continued by act of laſt ſeſſion to the year 1786.

† In the year 1743.

‡ Com. Jourg. 16 Vol. 369, 389.

fending the linens from Ireland to England has been computed at four per cent. and, if this computation is right, when the Britiſh linens obtain 12l. per cent. the full amount of the premium, the Iriſh do not receive above eight. Thofe bounties, though acknowledged to be a favour to Ireland, give Great-Britain a further, and a very important advantage in this trade, by inducing us to fend all our linens to England, from whence other countries are fupplied,

The great hinge upon which the ſtipulation on the part of England in the year 1698 turned, was that England ſhould give every poſſible encouragement to the linen and hempen manufactures in Ireland. Encouraging thefe manufactures in another country was not compatible with this intention. The courfe of events made it neceffary to do this in Scotland *; the courfe of trade

* To pleafe the Englifh Scotland has for half a century paſt exerted herfelf, as much as poſſible, to improve the linen manufacture. Anderfon on Induſtry, 2 Vol. 233.

trade made it neceffary for England to do
the fame; a commercial country muft cultivate every confiderable manufacture of
which fhe has or can get the primum.
Thefe circumftances have totally changed
the ftate of the queftion; and if it was
reafonable and juft that Ireland[1] in 1698
fhould have accepted of the linen in the
place of the woollen manufactures, it de-
ferves to be confidered, whether by the almoft total change of the circumftances it is
not now unreafonable and unjuft.

America itfelf, the opening of whofe
markets[1] to Irifh linens was thought to
have been one of the principal encouragements to that trade, is now become a rival
and an enemy, and when fhe puts off the
latter character will appear in the former
with new force and infinite advantages.

The emigrations for many years of fuch
great multitudes of our linen manufacturers

to

[1] Com. Journ. 16 vol. p. 370.

to America * proves incontrovertibly that they
can carry on their trade with more fuccefs
in America than in Ireland. But let us exa-
mine the facts to determine whether the
propofed encouragements have taken place.
The declaration of the lords of England
for the encouragement of the linen manufacture of Ireland was, " to all the
" advantage and profit that kingdom can be
" capable of," and of the commons, " that
" they fhall be *always* ready to give it their
" *utmoft* affiftance." The fpeech of the
lords juftices fhews the extent of this en-
gagement, and promifes the encouragement
of England, " to the linen and hempen
" manufactures of Ireland."

In the year 1705† liberty was given to the
natives of England or Ireland, to export
from Ireland to the Englifh plantations
white and brown linens only, but no liberty
given

* The province of Ulfter in two years is faid to have
loft 30.000 of its inhabitants. Com. Journ. 16 v. 381.

† From 24th June 1705. 3 and 4 Ann ch. 8. for 11
years; but afterwards continued.

given to bring in return any goods from
thence to Ireland, which will appear, from
the account in the appendix, to have made
this law of inconfiderable effect.   In 1743
premiums were given on the exportation of
Englifh and Irifh linens from Great Britain,
and the bounty granted by Great Britain in
1774, on flax-feed imported into Ireland, is a
further proof of the munificent attention
of Great Britain to our linen trade.   But
checquered, ftriped, printed, painted, ftain-
ed or dyed linens were not until lately admitted into the plantations from Ireland;
and the ftatutes of queen Anne*, laying
duties at the rate of 30 per cent on fuch
linens made in *foreign* parts and imported
into Great Britain, have been, rather by a
forced conftruction, extended to Ireland,
which is deprived of the Britifh markets†
for thofe goods, and, until the year 1777‡,
was excluded from the American markets
alfo.

* Brit. acts, 10 Anne, ch. 19. 11 and 12 Anne, ch. 9.
6 G. 1, ch. 4.
† Brit. act, 18 G. 3, ch. 53.
‡ Ir. Com. Journ. 16 vol. 363, 364.

alfo.. But it is thought as to chccqucred and
ftriped lincns, which arc a valuable branch
of the linen trade, that this act will have
little effect in favour of this country, from
the operation of the before-mentioned
Britifh act of the 10th G. 3, which, by granting a bounty on the exportation of thofe
goods of the manufacture of Great Britain
only, gives a direct preference to the Britifh
linen manufacture before the Irifh.

- The hempen manufacture of Ireland has
been fo far *difcouraged* by Great Britain, that
the Irifh have totally abandoned the culture
of hemp*.

I hope to be excufed for weighing fcru-
puloufly a propofed equivalent, for which
the receiver was obliged to part with the
advantages of which he was poffeffed.
The equivalent, given in 1667 for the almoft
entire exclufion of Ireland from the ports of
England and America, was the exportation
of

* Ir. Com. Journ. 16 vol. 365.

of our manufactures to foreign nations.
The prohibition of 1699 was not altogether
confiftent with the equivalent of 1667; and
from the equivalent of 1698 the fuperior
encouragement fince given to Englifh and
Scotch linen, and the difcouragement to the
checquer and ftamped linen and fail cloth
of Ireland muft make a large deduction. But
why muft one manufacture only be encouraged? the linen and the woollen trades of
Ireland were formerly both encouraged by
the legiflatures of both kingdoms; they are
now both equally encouraged in England.

If this fingle trade was found fufficient
employment for 1,000,000 men who remained in this country at the time of this reftraint (the contrary of which has been
fhewn), it would require the interpofition
of more than human wifdom to divide it
among 2,500,000 men at this day, and to
fend the multitude away fatisfied.

No populous commercial country can
fubfift on one manufacture; if the would
has

has ever produced fuch an inftance, I have not been able to find it. Reafon and experience demonftrate that, to make a fociety happy, the members of it muft be able to fupply the wants of each other, as far as their country affords the means, and where it does not, by exchanging the produce of their induftry for that of their neighbours. Where the former is difcouraged or the latter prevented, that community cannot be happy. If they are not allowed to fend to other countries the manufactured produce of their own, the people who enjoy that liberty will underfell them in their own markets; the reftrained manufacturers will be reduced to poverty, and will hang like paralytic limbs on the reft of the body.

If England's commercial fyftem would have been incomplete, had fhe failed to cultivate any one principal manufacture of which fhe had or could obtain the material, what fhall we fay to the commercial ftate of that country, reftrained in a manufacture of which fhe has the materials in

L   abundance,

bundance, and in which fhe had made great progrefs, and almoft confined to one manufacture of which fhe has not the primum.

Manufactures, though they may flourifh for a time, generally fail in countries that do not produce the principal materials of them. Of this there are many inftances. Venice and the other Italian ftates carried on the woollen manufacture, until the countries which produced the materials manufactured them, when the Italian manufactures declined, and dwindled into little confideration in comparifon of their former fplendor. The Flemings, from their vicinity to thofe countries that produced the materials, beat the Italians out of their markets. But when England cultivated that manufacture, the Flemings loft it. That this and not oppreffion was the caufe appears from the flourifhing ftate of the linen manufacture* there, becaufe it confumes flax the

native

---

* Anderfon on Induftry, 1 vol. 34 to 40.

native produce of the foil; and it is much
to be feared that thofe iflands will be obliged to yield the fuperiority in this trade to
other nations that have great extent of
country, and fufficient land to fpare for
this impoverifhing production.

That fome parts of Ireland may produce
good flax muft be allowed, and alfo that
parts of Flanders would produce fine wool.
But though the legiflature has for many
years made it a capital object to encourage
the growth of flax and the raifing of flax-
feed in this kingdom, yet it is obliged to
pay above 9000l. yearly in premiums on
the importation of flax-feed, which is now
almoft all imported, and cofts us between 70
and 80,000l. yearly. Flax-farming, in any
large quantity, is become a precarious and
lofing trade†, and thofe who have been induced to attempt it by premiums from the
linen-board have, after receiving thofe pre-

L 2   miums,

---

† Com. Journ. 16 vol. 370.

miums, generally found themfelves lofers,
and have declined that branch of tillage.

When the imported flax-feed is unfound
and fails in particular diftricts, which very
frequently happens, the diftrefs, confufion
and litigation that arife among manufacturers, farmers, retailers and merchants, affords a melancholy proof of the dangerous
confequences to a populous nation, when
the induftry of the people, and the hope of
the rifing year reft on a fingle manufacture,
for the materials of which we muft depend
upon the courtefy and good faith of other
nations.

Let me appeal to the experience of very
near a century, in the very inftance now
before you. A fingle manufacture is highly
encouraged; it obtains large premiums not
only from the legiflature of its own country, but from that of a great neighbouring
kingdom; it becomes not only the firft, but
almoft the fole national object; immenfe
fums of money are expended in the cultivation

tion of it §, and the fuccefs exceeds our moft fanguine expectations. But look into the ftate of this country; you will find property circulating flowly and languidly, and in the moft numerous claffes of your people, no circulation or property at all. You will frequently find them in want of employment and of food, and reduced in a vaft number of inftances from the flighteft caufes to diftrefs and beggary. All other manufacturers will continue fpiritlefs, poor and diftreffed, and derive from uncertain employment a precarious and miferable fub-fiftence; they gain little by the fuccefs of the profperous trade; the dealers in which are tempted to buy from that country to which they principally fell; the difeafe of thofe morbid parts muft fpread through the whole body, and will at length reach the perfons employed in the favoured manufacture. Thefe will become poor and wretched and difcontented; they emigrate by thoufands; in vain you reprefent the crime of deferting

<hr/>

§ See Com. Jour. 17 vol. 263 to 287 for the fums paid from 1700 to 1775. They amount to 803,486l os 2½d

deferting their country, the folly of forfaking their friends, the temerity of wandering to diftant and perhaps inhofpitable climates; their defpondency is deaf to the fuggeftions of prudence, and will anfwer, that they can no longer ftay " where hope never comes," but will fly from thefe " regions of forrow*."

Let me not be thought to undervalue the bounties and generofity of that great nation which has taken our linen trade under its protection. There is much ill-breeding, though perhaps fome good fenfe, in the churlifh reply of the philofopher to the requeft of the prince who vifited his humble dwelling, and defired to know, and to gratify his wifhes; they were no more than this, that the prince fhould not ftand between the philofopher and the fun. Had he been a man of the world he might have exprefled the fame idea with more ad-drefs, though with lefs force and fignificance; he

---

* This malady of emigration among our linen manu-facturers has appeared at many different periods during this century.

he might have faid, " I am fenfible of your
" greatnefs and of your power; I have no
" doubts of your liberality ; but Nature has
" abundantly given me all that I wifh ; in-
" tercept not one of her greateft gifts;
" allow me to enjoy the bounties of her
" hand, and the contentment of my own
" mind will furnifh the reft."

I have the honour to be,

My lord, &c.

T H E

T H E

COMMERCIAL RESTRAINTS

O F

I R E L A N D

C O N S I D E R E D.

S E V E N T H   L E T T E R.

THE

COMMERCIAL RESTRAINTS

OF

IRELAND

CONSIDERED.

SEVENTH LETTER.

My Lord,

Dublin, 3d Sept. 1779.

BY comparing the reftrictive law of 1699, with the ftatutes which had been previoufly enacted in England from the 15th year of the reign of Charles the fecond, relative to the Colonies, it appears that this reftrictive law originated in a fyftem of colonization. The principle of that fyftem was that the Colonies fhould fend their materials to England and take from thence her manufactures, and that the making thofe manufactures in the Colonies fhould be prohibited

hibited or difcouraged. But was it reafonable to extend this principle to Ireland? the
climate, growth and productions of the Colonies were different from thofe of their
parent country. England had no fugar
canes, coffee, dying ftuff, and little tobacco.
She took all thofe from her Colonies only,
and it was thought reafonable that they
fhould take from her only the manufactures
which fhe made. But in Ireland, the climate, foil, growth and productions are the
fame as in England, who could give no
fuch equivalent to Ireland as fhe gave to
America, and was fo far from confidering
her, when this fyftem firft prevailed, as a
proper fubject for fuch regulations, that
fhe was allowed the benefits arifing from
thofe Colonies equally with England, until
the 15th year of the reign of king Charles *
the fecond. By an act paffed in that year
Ireland had no longer the privilege of fending any of her exports, except fervants,
horfes, victuals and falt, to any of the Colonies;

* 15 Ch. II. ch. 7.

nies; the reafons arc affigned in the preamble, " to make this kingdom a ftaple, not
" only of the commodities of thofe planta-
" tions, but alfo of the commodities of other
" countries and places for the fupplying of
" them, and it being the ufage of other na-
" tions to keep their plantation trade to
" themfelves *." At the time of paffing this
law, though lefs liberal ideas in refpc&of Ireland were then entertained, it went no further than not to extend to her the benefit of thofe Colony regulations; but it was
not then thought that this kingdom was a
proper fubjec& for any fuch regulations.
The fcheme of fubftituting there, inftead of
the woollen, the linen trade, was not at that
time thought of. The Englifh were defir-
ous to eftablifh it among themfelves, and
by an a& of parliament† made in that year
for encouraging the manufacture of linen,
granted to all foreigners who fhall fet it up
in

* As other nations did the fame, Ireland was fhut out
from the new world, and a confiderable part of the old in
Afia and Africa.

† 15 Ch. II. ch. 15.

in England, the privileges of natural born
fubjects.

But it appears by the Englifh ftatute of
the 7th and 8th Will. III*. which has been
before ftated, that this fcheme had not fuc-
ceeded in England, and from this act it is
manifeft that England confidered itfelf as well
as Ireland interefted to encourage the linen-
manufacture there; and it does not then appear to have been thought juft, that Ireland
fhould purchafe this benefit for both, by
giving up the exportation of any other manufacture. But in 1698 a different principle
prevailed; in effect the fame, fo far as relates to the woollen manufacture, with that
which had prevailed as to the commerce of
the Colonies. This is evident from the preamble of the Englifh law † made in 1699,
" for as much as wool and woollen manu-
" factures of cloth, ferge, bays, kerfies and
" other ftuffs, made or mixed with wool,
                                    " are

* Ch. 39.
† 10th and 11th W. III. ch. 10.

" are the greateſt, and moſt profitable com-
" modities of this kingdom, on which the
" value of lands and the trade of the nation
" do chiefly depend, and whereas great quan-
" tities of like manufactures have of late
" been made and are daily encreaſing in the
" kingdom of Ireland, and *in the Engliſh*
" *plantations* in America, and are exported
" from thence to foreign markets, hereto-
" fore ſupplied from England, which will
" inevitably ſink the value of lands, and
" tend to the ruin of the trade and woollen
" manufactures of this realm; for the pre-
" vention whereof and for the encourage-
" ment of the woollen manufactures in this
" kingdom, &c."

The ruinous conſequences of the woollen
manufactures of Ireland to the value of
lands, trade and manufactures of England,
ſtated in this act, are apprehenſions that
were entertained, and not events that had
happened; and before thoſe facts are taken
for granted, I requeſt the miſchiefs recited
in

in the acts * made in England to prevent the importation of cattle dead or
alive from Ireland, may be confidered. The
mifchiefs ftated in thofe feveral laws are
fuppofed to be as ruinous to England as
thofe recited in the act of 1699, and yet are
now allowed to be groundlefs apprehenfions,
occafioned by fhort and miftaken views of the
real intereft of England. Sir W. Petty † de-
monftrates that the opinion entertained in
England at the time of his prohibition of
the import of cattle from Ireland was ill-
founded; he calls it a ftrange conceit. If he
was now living, he would probably confider
the prohibition of our woollen exports as
not having a much better foundation.

Connecting

* 15 Ch. II. ch. 7. 18 Ch. II. ch. 2. 20 Ch. II. ch. 7.
22d and 23d Ch. II. ch. 2. 32 Ch. II. ch. 2.

† Petty's Political Survey of Ireland, 70 ; and ib. Report
from the Council of Trade, 117, 118.

Sir W. Temple, 3 Vol. p. 22, 23, that England was evidently a lofer by the prohibition of Cattle.

Dr. Smith's Memoirs of Wool, 2 Vol. 337. that
the Englifh had fince fufficiently felt the mifchiefs of this
proceeding.

Connecting this preamble of the act of 1699, with the fpeech made from the throne to the parliament of Ireland in the year 1698, with the addreffes of both houfes in England, and with the prohibition, by this and by other acts formerly made in England, of exporting wool from Ireland except to that kingdom, the object of this new commercial regulation is obvious. It was to difcourage the woollen manufacture in Ireland, and in effect, to prohibit the exportation from thence, becaufe it was the principal branch of manufacture and trade in England, to induce us to fend to them our materials for that manufacture, and that we fhould be fupplied with it by them, and to encourage, as a compenfation to Ireland, the linen manufacture, which was not at that time a commercial object of any importance to England. This I take to be a part of the fyftem of colony regulations. Whether it was reafonable or juft to bring this kingdom into that fyftem, has been already fubmitted from arguments drawn from the climates and productions of the different

M   countries.

countries. The fuppofed compenfation was
no more than what Ireland had before; no
further encouragement was given by England to our linen manufacture until fix years
after this prohibition, when at the requeft
of the Irifh houfe of commons, and after a
reprefentation of the ruinous ftate of this
country, liberty was given by an Englifh act
of parliament * to export our white and
brown linens into the colonies, which was
allowing us to do as to one manufacture
what, before the 15th of king Charles the
fecond, was permitted in every inftance.

It would be prefumption in a private
man to decide on the weight of thofe arguments; but to felect and arrange facts that
lie difperfed in journals and books of ftatutes in both kingdoms, and to make obfervations on thofe facts with caution and refpect, can never give offence to thofe who
inquire for the purpofe of relieving a diftreffed

* 3 and 4 Ann. ch. 8.

treffed nation, and of promoting the general welfare.

In that confidence I beg leave to place this fubject in a different view, and to requeft that it may be confidered what the commercial fyftem of this kingdom was at the time of paffing this law of 1699? and whether it was, in this refpect, reafonable or juft that fuch a regulation fhould have been then made? The great object which the lords and commons of Great Britain have determined to inveftigate lead to fuch a difcuffion; determined as they are to purfue effectual methods " for promoting " the common ftrength, wealth and com- " merce of both kingdoms," what better guides can they follow than the examples of their anceftors, and the means ufed by them for many centuries, and in the happieft times, for attaining the fame great purpofes.

In my opinion it would be improper, in the prefent ftate of the Britifh empire, to

M 2   agitate

agitate difputed queftions that may enflame the paffions of men. May no fuch
queftions ever arife between two affectionate fifter kingdoms! It is my purpofe only
to ftate acknowledged facts, which never
have been contefted, and from thofe facts
to lay before you the commercial fyftem of
Ireland before the year 1699.

For feveral centuries before this period
Ireland was in poffeffion of the Englifh common law *, and of magna charta. The former fecures the fubject in the enjoyment of
property of every kind; and by the latter
*the liberties of all the ports of the kingdom are
eftablifhed.*

The ftatutes made in England for the
common and public weal, are † by an Irifh
act of the 10th of Henry the 7th, made
laws

---

* 4 Inft. 349. Matth. Paris, anno 1172. p. 121, 220.
Vit. H. 2. Pryn. againft the 4th Inft. c. 76, p. 250, 252.
Sir John Davis's Hift. 71. Lord Lyttleton's Hift. of H. 2.
3 Vol. 89, 90. 7 Co. 22. 23. 4th Black. 429.

Cooke's 4th Inft. 351.

laws in Ireland; and the Englifh commercial ftatutes, in which Ireland is exprefsly mentioned, will place the former ftate of commerce in this country in a light very different from that in which it has been generally confidered in Great-Britain.

By the 17th of Edward the 3d, ch. 1. all forts of merchandizes may be exported from Ireland, except to the king's enemies.

By the 27th of Edward the 3d, ch. 18. merchants of Ireland and Wales may bring their merchandize to the ftaple of England; and by the 34th of the fame king, ch. 17. all kinds of merchandizes may be exported from and imported into Ireland, as well by aliens as denizens. In the fame year there is another ftatute, ch. 18. that all perfons who have lands or poffeffions in Ireland, might freely import thither, and export from that kingdom *their own commodities*; and by the 50th of Edward the 3d, ch. 8. no alnage is to be paid, if frize ware, which are made in Ireland.

This

This freedom of commerce was beneficial to both countries. It enabled Ireland to be very ferviceable to Edward the 3d, as it had been to his father and grandfather, in fupplying numbers of armed veffels for tranfporting their great lords and their attendants and troops * to Scotland, and alfo to Portfmouth for his French wars.

But the reign of Edward the 4th furnifhes ftill ftronger inftances of the regard fhewn by England to the trade and manufactures of this country.

In the third year of that monarch's reign the artificers of England complained to parliament that they were greatly impoverifhed and *could not live* by bringing in divers commodities and wares ready wrought +. An act paffed reciting thofe complaints and ordaining that no merchant born a fubject of the king, denizen or ftranger, or other perfon fhould bring into England or Wales any

* Anderfon on Commerce, 1 Vol. 174.
+ 3d Edw. 4. ch. 4.

any woollen cloths, &c. and enumerates many other manufactures, on pain of forfeiture; provided that all wares and "chaf-" "fers" made and wrought in Ireland or Wales, may be brought in and fold in t'e realm of England, as they were wont before the making of that act *.

In the next year another act † paffed in that kingdom, that all woollen cloth brought into England and fet to fale, fhould be forfeited, except cloths made in Wales or Ireland.

In thofe reigns England was as careful of the commerce and manufactures of her ancient fifter kingdom, particularly in her great ftaple trade, as fhe was of her own.

Of this attention there were further inftances in the years 1468 and 1478. In two treaties

* The part of this law which mentions that it fhall be determinable at the king's pleafure, has the prohibition for its object, and does not leffen the force of the argument in favour of Ireland.

† 4th Edw. IV. ch. 1.

treaties concluded in thofe years between
England and the duke, of Bretagne, the
merchandize to be traded in between England, Ireland and Calais on the one part,
and Bretagne on the other, is fpecified, and
woollen cloths are particularly mentioned *.

And in a treaty between Henry the 7th
and the Netherlands, Ireland is included,
both as to exports and imports †.

The commercial acts of parliament in
which Ireland is mentioned have only been
ftated, becaufe they are not generally known.
But the laws made in England before the
10th of Henry the 7th, for the protection
of merchants and the fecurity of trade, being laws for the common and public weal,
are alfo made laws here by the Irifh ftatute
of that year, which was returned under the
great feal of England, and muft have been
previoufly confidered in the privy council of
that kingdom. At this period then the
                                        Englifh

* Anderfon on Commerce, 1 Vol. 285.
† Ib. 319.

Englifh commercial fyftem and the Irifh, fo far as it depended upon the Englifh ftatute law, was the fame ; and before this period, fo far as it depended upon the common law and Magna Charta, was alfo the fame.

From that time until t'e 15th of king Charles the 2d, which takes in a period of 167 years, the commercial conftitution of Ireland was as much favoured and protected as that of England ; " the free enlargement " of common traffick which his majefty's ". fubjects of Ireland enjoyed," is taken notice of, incidentally, in an Englifh ftatute, in the reign of king James the 1ft * ; and in 1627 king Charles the 1ft made a ftrong declaration in favour of the trade and manufactures of this country. By feveral Englifh ftatutes in the reign of king Charles the 2d, an equal attention was fhewn to the woollen manufactures in both kingdoms; in the 12th year of his reign† the exportation of wool, wool-felts, fuller's earth, or any kind of

* 3d James, ch. 6.
† 12th Ch. 2, ch. 32.

of fcowering-earth, was prohibited from both. But let the reafons, mentioned in the preamble, for paffing this law be adverted to, —" for preventing inconveniencies " and loffes that happened, and that daily " do and may happen to the kingdom of " England, dominion of Wales, and king- " dom of Ireland, through the fecret expor- " tation of wool out of and from the faid " kingdoms and dominions; and for the *better* " *fetting on work the poor people* and inhabi- " tants of the kingdoms and dominions " aforefaid, and to the intent that the full " ufe and benefit of *the principal native com-* " *modities* of the fame kingdom and domini- " on may come, redound and be unto the " fubjects and inhabitants of the fame:"

This was the voice of nature, and the dictate of found and general policy; it proclaimed to the nations that they fhould not give to ftrangers the bread of their own children, that the produce of the foil fhould fupport the inhabitants of the country, that their induftry fhould be exercifed on their

own

own materials, and that the poor fhould be employed, clothed and fed.

The fhipping and navigation of England and Ireland were at this time equally favoured and protected. By another act of the fame year no goods or commodities † of the growth, production or manufacture of Afia, Africa or America, fhall be imported into England, *Ireland* or Wales, but in fhips which belong to the people of England or *Ireland*, the dominion of Wales, or the town of Berwick upon Tweed, or which are of the built of the faid lands, and of which the mafter and three-fourths of the mariners are Englifh; and a fubfequent ftatute * makes the encouragement to navigation in both countries equal, by ordaining that the fubjects of Ireland and of the Plantations fhall be accounted Englifh within the meaning of that claufe. Another law‡ of the fame reign fhews that the navigation

† 12 Ch. 2, ch. 18.
* 13th and 14th Ch. 2, ch. 11.
‡ 13th and 14th Ch. 2, ch. 18.

vigation, commerce and woollen manufactures of both kingdoms were equally protected by the Englifh legiflature. This act lays on the fame reftraint as the abovementioned act of the 12th of Charles 2d. and makes the tranfgreffion ftill more penal. It recites that wool, wool-felts, &c. are fecretly exported from England and Ireland to foreign parts to the great decay of the woollen manufactures and the deftruction of the navigation and commerce of *thefe kingdoms*.

From thofe laws it appears that the commerce, navigation and manufactures of this country were not only favoured and protected by the Englifh legiflature, but that we had in thofe times the full benefit of their Plantation trade; whilft the woollen manufactures were protected and encouraged in England and Ireland, the planting of tobacco in both was prohibited, becaufe "it "was one of the main products of feveral "of the plantations, and upon which their welfare

" welfare and fubfiftence do depend †. This policy was liberal, juft and equal, it opened the refources and cultivated the ftrength of every part of the empire.

This commercial fyftem of Ireland was enforced by feveral acts of her own legifla-ture; two ftatutes paffed in the reign of Henry the 8th to prevent the exportation of wool, becaufe, fays the firft of thofe laws, " it hath been the caufe of dearth of " cloth and idlenefs of many folks *," and " tends to the defolation and ruin of this " poor land." The fecond of thofe laws in-forces the prohibition § by additional penal-ties; it recites, " that the faid beneficial " law had taken little effect, but that fince " the making thereof great plenty of wool " had been conveyed out of this land to the " great and ineftimable hurt, decay and im-" poverifhment of the king's poor fubjects " within the faid land, for redrefs whereof " and in confideration that conveying of the " wool

---

† 12 Ch. 2, ch. 27.
* Ir. act, 13 H. 8, ch. 2. § 28 H. 8, ch. 17.

" wool of the growth of this land out of
" the fame is one of the greateft occafions
" of the idlenefs of the people, wafte, ruin
" and defolation of the king's cities and bo-
" rough towns, and other places of his do-
" minion within this land." The 11th of
Elizabeth* lays duties on the exportation
equal to a prohibition; and the reafon given
in the preamble ought to be mentioned;
" that the faid commodities may be more
" abundantly wrought in this realm ere they
" fhall be fo tranfported, than prefently they
" are, which fhall fet many now living idle
" on work, to the great relief and commodity
" of this realmt.

By the preamble of one of thofe acts §,
made in the reign of Charles the Second, it
appears that the fale of Irifh woollen goods
in

---

* Ch. 10.

† The neceffity of encouraging the people of Ireland
to manufacture their own wool, appears by divers ftatutes
to have been the fenfe of the legiflature of both kingdoms
for fome centuries.

§ Ir. Act of 17 and 18 Ch. 2, ch. 15.

in foreign markets was encouraged by England; " whereas there is a general complaint
" in *England*, France, and other parts be-
" yond the feas, (whither the woollen cloths
" and other commodities made of wool in
" this his majefty's kingdom of Ireland are
" tranfported) of the falfe, deceitful, uneven,
" and uncertain making thereof, which com-
" eth to pafs by reafon that the clothiers
" and makers thereof do not obferve any
" certain affize for length, breath and
" weight for making their clothes and other
" commodities aforefaid in this kingdom, as
" they do in the realm of England, and as
" they ought alfo to do here; by which
" means the merchants, buyers and ufers of
" the faid cloth and other commodities are
" much abufed and deceived, and the credit,
" efteem and fale of the faid cloth and com-
" modities is thereby much impaired and un-
" dervalued, to the great and general hurt
" and hindrance of the trade of clothing in
" this whole realm."

After

After the ports of England were fhut a-gainft our cattle, and our trade to the Eng-lifh colonies was reftrained, ftill this com-mercial fyftem was adhered to by encourag-ing the manufactures of this country, and the exportation of them to foreign countries. In 1667, when the power of the crown was not fo well underftood as at prefent, the proclamation before mentioned was publifh-ed by the lord lieutenant and privy council of Ireland *, in purfuance of a letter from Charles the Second, by the advice of his council in England, notifying to all his fubjects of this kingdom, the allowance of a free trade to all foreign countries, either at war or peace with his majefty.

In the year 1663 the diftinctions between the trade of England and Ireland †, and the reftraints on that of the latter commenced. By an Englifh act paffed in that year, in-titled an act " for the encouragement of " trade,"

* Carte, 2 Vol. p. 344.
† 15 Ch. 2, ch. 7.

"trade," a title not very applicable to the
parts of it that related to Ireland, befides
laying a duty nearly equal to a prohibition
on cattle imported into England from that
kingdom, the exportation of all commodities, except victuals, fervants, horfes, and
falt for the fifheries of New England and
Newfoundland, from thence to the Englifh
plantations, was prohibited from the 25th
of March, 1764. The exports allowed
were ufeful to them, but prejudicial to Ireland, as they confifted of our people, our
provifions, and a material for manufacture
which we might have ufed more profitably
on our own coafts.

In 1670 another act * paffed in England,
to prohibit from the 24th of March 1671
the exportation from the Englifh plantations
to Ireland of feveral materials for manufactures †, without firft unloading in England

N   or

22d and 23d Ch. 2d, ch. 26.
† Sugar, tobacco, cotton, wool, indigo, fteel or Ja-
maica wood, fuftick, or other dying wood, the growth
of the faid plantations.

or Wales. We are informed by this act that the reftraint of the exportation from the Englifh plantations to Ireland was intended by the act of 1663 ; but the intention is not effectuated, though the importation of thofe commodities into Ireland *from England*, without firft unloading there, is, in effect, prohibited by that act.

The prohibition of importing into Ireland any plantation goods, unlefs the fame had been firft landed in England, and had paid the duties, is made general, without any exception, by the Englifh act of the 7th and 8th W. 3d, ch. 22.

But by fubfequent Britifh acts *, it is made lawful to import from his majefty's plantations, all goods of their growth or manufactures, the articles enumerated in thofe feveral acts excepted †.

By

* 4 Geo. 2, ch. 15. 6 G. 2, ch. 15. 4 G. 2, ch. 15.
† The articles in the laft note, and alfo rice, molaffes, beaver fkins and other furs, copper ore, pitch, tar, turpentine,

By a late British act‡ there is a confiderable extenfion of the exports from Ireland
to the Britifh plantations. But it is apprehended that this law will not anfwer the
kind intentions of the Britifh legiflature.
Denying the import from thofe countries to
Ireland, is, in effect, preventing the export

N 2   from

tine, mafts, yards and bowfprits, pimento, cocoa nuts,
whale fins, raw filk, hides and fkins, pot and pearl afhes,
iron and lumber.

‡ From the 24th of June 1778, it fhall be lawful to
export from Ireland directly into any of the Britifh plantations in America, or the Weft Indies, or into any of the
fettlements belonging to Great Britain on the coaft of
Africa, any goods being the produce or manufacture of
Ireland (wool and woollen manufactures in all its branches,
mixed or unmixed, cotton manufactures of all forts mixed
or unmixed, hats, glafs, hops, gun-powder and coals,
only excepted) and all goods, &c. of the growth, produce
or manufacture of Great Britain, which may be legally
imported from thence into Ireland (woollen manufactures
in all its branches, and glafs, excepted) and all foreign cer-
tificate goods that may be legally imported from Great
Britain into Ireland. Two of the principal manufactures
are excepted, and one of them clofely connected with, if
not a part of the linen manufacture.—18 Geo. 3, ch.
55.

from Ireland to thofe countries. Money
cannot be expeded for our goods there;
we muft take theirs in exchange, and this
can never anfwer on the terms of our being obliged, in our return, to pafs by Ireland, to land thofe goods in England, to fhip
them a fecond time, and then to fail back
again to Ireland. No trade will bear fuch
an unneceffary delay and expence. The
quicknefs and the fecurity of the return
are the great inducements to every trade.
One is loft and the other hazarded by fuch
embarraffments; thofe who are not fubjcd
to them carry on the trade with fuch advantages over thofe who are fo entangled,
as totally to exclude them from it. This
is no longer the fubjcd of fpeculation, it
has been proved by the experience of above
feventy years. Since the year 1705, when
liberty was given to import white and brown
linens from Ireland into the Englifh plantations, the quantities fent there diredly
from Ireland were at all times very inconfiderable ; notwithftanding this liberty they
were fent for the moft part from Ireland to
England,

England, before any bounty was given on
the exportation from thence, which did not
take place until the year 1743, and from
England the Englifh plantations were fupplied. There cannot be a more decifive
proof that the liberty of exporting without
a direct import in return, will not be beneficial to Ireland.

This country is the part of the Britifh
empire moft conveniently fituated for trade
with the colonies ; if not fuffered to have
any beneficial intercourfe with them, fhe
will be deprived of one of the great advantages of her fituation ; and fuch an ob-
ftruction to the profperity of fo confiderable a part, muft neceffarily diminifh the
ftrength of the whole Britifh empire.

Thofe laws laid Ireland under reftraints
highly prejudicial to her commerce and navigation. From thofe countries the materials for fhip-building *, and fome of thofe
ufed

* This appears by the Englifh acts (3 and 4 Ann. ch. 10.
8 Ann. ch. 13. 2 Geo 2d, ch. 35.) giving bounties on the
importation of thofe articles into Great Britain

used in perfecting their staple manufactures
were had; Ireland was by those laws excluded from almost all the trade of three quar-
ters of the globe, and from all direct beneficial intercourse with her fellow-subjects
in those countries, which were partly stock-
ed from her own loins. But still, though
deprived at that time of the benefit of those
colonies, she was not then considered as a
colony herself; her manufacturers were not
in any other manner discouraged, her ports
were left open, and she was at liberty to
look for a market among strangers, though
not among her fellow-subjects in Asia,
Africa or America *. By the law of 1699
she

* Sir William Petty mentions that " the English who have
" lands in Ireland were forced to trade only with strangers,
" and became unacquainted with their own country, and
" that England gained more than it lost by a free com-
" merce (with Ireland), as exporting hither three times
" as much as it received from hence ;" and mentions his
surprize at their being debarred from bringing commodities from America directly home, and being obliged to
bring them round from England with extreme hazard and
loss.—Political Survey of Ireland, p. 123.

fhe was, as to her ftaple manufacture, deprived of thofe refources ; fhe was brought
within a fyftem of colonization, but on
worfe terms than any of the plantations who
were allowed to trade with each other †.

She could fend her principal materials
for manufacture to England only ; but thofe
manufactures were encouraged in England
and difcouraged in Ireland. The probable
confequence of which was, and the event
has anfwered the expectation, that we
fhould take thofe manufactures from that
country, and that therefore in thofe various
trades which employ the greateft numbers
of men, the Englifh fhould work for our
people. The rich fhould work for the
poor !

Let the hiftories of both kingdoms, and
the ftatute books of both parliaments be
examined, and no precedent will be found
for

† 22d and 23d Ch. 2d, ch. 26. Sec. 11.

for the act of 1699, or for the fyftem which it introduced.

The whole tenor of the Englifh ftatutes relative to the trade of this country, and which by our act of the 10th of Hen. VII. became a part of our commercial conftitution, breath a fpirit totally repugnant to the principle of that law, and it is therefore with the utmoft deference fubmitted to thofe who have the power to decide, whether this law was agreeable to the commercial conftitution of Ireland, which for 500 years has never produced a fimilar inftance.

It might be naturally fuppofed, by a perfon not verfed in our ftory, that in the feventeenth century there had been fome offence given, or fome demerit on our part. He would be furprized to hear that during this period our loyalty had been exemplary, and our fufferings on that account great. In 1641, great numbers of the proteftants of Ireland were deftroyed, and many of them were

were deprived of their property, and driven out of their country from their attachment to the Englifh government in this kingdom, and to that religion and conftitution which they happily enjoyed under it. At the revolution they were conftant in the fame principles, and fuccefsfully ftaked their lives and properties againft domeftick and foreign enemies, in fupport of the rights of the Englifh crown, and of the religious and civil liberties of Britain and of Ireland. They bravely fhared with her in all her dangers, and liberally partook of all her adverfities. Whatever were their rights they had forfeited none of them. Whatever favours they enjoyed, they had new claims, from their merit and their fufferings, to a continuance of them. They now wanted more than ever the care of that foftering hand, which by refcuing them twice from oppreffion (obligations never to be forgotten by the proteftants of Ireland) eftablifhed the liberties, confirmed the ftrength, and raifed the glory of the Britifh empire.

In

In fpeaking of a commercial fyftem it is not intended to touch upon the power of making or altering laws; the prefent fubject leads us only to confider whether that power has been exercifed, in any inftances, contrary to reafon, juftice, and public utility,

When we confider, with the utmoft deference to eftablifhed authority, what is *reafonable, ufeful and juft*, principles equally applicable to an independent or a fubordinate, to a rich or a poor country—

Quod æque pauperibus prodeft, locupletibus æque.—

Should any man talk of a conqueft above 500 years fince, between kingdoms long united, like thofe, in blood, intereft and conftitution, he does not fpeak to the purpofe ; he may as well talk of the conqueft of the Norman, and ufe the antiquated language of obfolete defpotifm. I revere that conqueft which has given to Ireland

the

the common law and the Magna Charta of England.

When we confider what is *reasonable*, *use-ful and just*, and addrefs our fentiments to a nation renowned for wifdom and juftice, fhould pride pervert the queftion, talk of the power of Britain, and in the character of that great country, afk, like Tancred, who fhall controul me ? I anfwer, like the fober Siffredi——*thyself*.

The power of regulating trade in a great empire is perverted, when exercifed for the deftruction of trade in any part of it; but whatever or wherever that power is, if it fays to the fubject on one fide of a channel, you may work and navigate, buy and fell; and to the fubject on the other fide, you fhall not work or navigate, buy or fell, but under fuch reftrictions as will extinguifh the geni-us, and unnerve the arm of induftry; I will only fay that it ufes a language repugnant to the free fpirit of commerce, and of the Britifh and Irifh conftitution.

Great

Great eulogiums on the virtues of our people have been pronounced by fome of the moft refpected Englifh authors *; yet indolence is objected to them by thofe who difcourage their induftry; but they do not reflect that each of thefe proceeds from habit, and that the noble obfervation made on virtue in general is equally applicable to induftry—the day that it lofes its liberty half of its vigour is gone †.

The great expenditure of money by England, on account of this country, is an argument more fit for the limited views of a compting-houfe, than for the enlarged policy of ftatefmen deliberating on the general good of a great empire.

Very large fums, it is true, were advanced by England for the relief and recovery of Ireland; but thefe have been reimburfed fifty fold by the profits and advantages which

* Sir John Davis and Sir Edward Cooke.

† Νμισυ Γαρ Ιαρίϛ; ναπυαιντlαι Δυλιον ημαρ.

Homer, as quoted by Longinus.

which have fince arifen to England from its trade and intercourfe with this kingdom. This argument may be further purfued, but accounts of mutual benefits between intimate friends and, near relations fhould be always kept open, and every attempt to ftrike a balance between them tends rather to raife jealoufies than to promote good will.

It has been faid that the intereft of England required that thofe reftraints fhould be impofed. The contrary has been fhewn ; one of the maxims of her own law inftructs us to enjoy our own property fo as not to injure that of our neighbour * ; and the true intereft of a great country lies in the population, wealth and ftrength of the whole empire.

If this reftrictive fyftem was founded in juftice and found policy towards the middle and at the conclufion of the laft century, the prefent ftate of the Britifh empire requires new counfels, and a fyftem of commerce

* Sic utere tuo, alienum non Lædas.

merce and of policy totally different from thofe which the circumftances of thefe countries, in the years 1663, 1670 and 1698, might have fuggefted.

But it is time to give your lordfhip a little relief, before I enter into a new part of my fubject.

I have the honour to be,

My lord, &c.

THE

THE

COMMERCIAL RESTRAINTS

OF

IRELAND

CONSIDERED.

EIGHTH LETTER.

THE

COMMERCIAL RESTRAINTS

OF

IRELAND

CONSIDERED.

EIGHTH LETTER.

MY LORD,

Dublin, 6th September, 1779.

BETWEEN the 23d of October, 1641, and the fame day in the year 1652, five hundred and four thoufand of the inhabitants of Ireland are faid to have perifhed and been wafted by the fword, plague, famine, hardfhip and banifhment *. If it had not been for the numbers of Britifh which thofe wars had brought over †, and fuch who either as

O   adventurers

* Sir William Petty's Political Survey of Ireland, p. 19.
† Sir William Temple, 3 Vol. p 7.

adventurers or foldiers feated themfelves
here on account of the fatisfaction made to
them in lands, the country had been by the
rebellion of 1641, and the plague that followed it, nearly defolate. At the reftoration almoft the whole property of the kingdom was in a ftate of the utmoft anarchy
and confufion. To fatisfy the clafhing interefts of the numerous claimants, and to
determine the various and intricate difputes
that arofe relative to titles, required a confiderable length of time. Peace and fettlement, or, to ufe the words of one of the
acts of parliament * of that time, the repairing the ruins and defolation of the kingdom
were the great objects of this period.

The Englifh law † of 1663, reftraining the
exportation from Ireland to America, was at
that time, and for fome years after, fcarcely
felt in this kingdom, which had then little to
export except live cattle, not proper for fo
diftant a market.

The

* The act of Explanation.
† 15 Ch. II.

The act of fettlement paffed in Ireland the year before this reftrictive law, and the explanatory ftatute for the 'fettlement of this kingdom, was not enacted until two years after. The country continued for a confiderable time in a ftate of litigation, which is never favorable to induftry. In 1661 the people muft have been poor; the number of them of all degrees, who paid poll money in that year was about 360,000*. In 1672, when the country had greatly improved, the manufacture beftowed upon a year's exportation from Ireland, did not exceed eight thoufand pounds†, and the clothing trade had not then arrived to what it had been before the laft rebellion. But ftill the kingdom had much increafed in wealth, tho' not in manufactured exports. The cuftoms which fet in 1656 for 12,000l. yearly, were in 1672 worth 80,000l. ‡ yearly, and the improvement in domeftic wealth, that is to fay, in building, planting, furniture,

O 2   coaches,

* Sir W. Petty, p 9.
† Ib. 9. and 110.
‡ Ib. 89.

coaches, &c. is faid to have advanced from
1652 to 1673 in a proportion of from one to
four. Sir William Petty in the year 1672
complains not of the reftraints on the exportation from Ireland to America *, but of the
prohibition of exporting our cattle to England, and of our being obliged to unlade in
that kingdom † the fhips bound from America to Ireland; the latter regulation he
confiders as highly prejudicial to this country †.

The immediate object of Ireland at this
time, feems to have been to get materials to
employ her people at home without think-
ing of foreign exportations. When we advanced in the export of our woollen goods,
the law of 1663 ‡, which excluded them from
the American markets, muft have been a
great lofs to this kingdom; and after we
were allowed to export our linens to the
Britifh colonies in America, the reftraints
impofed

* Sir W. Petty, p. 9 and 10.
  Ib. 34, 71, 125.
‡ 15 Ch. II. ch. 7.

impofed by the law of 1670 upon our impor-
tations from thence became more prejudicial, and will be much more fo if ever the
late extenfion of our exports to America
fhould under thofe reftraints have any effect.
For it is certainly a great difcouragement to
the carrying on trade with any country
where we are allowed only to fell our
manufactures and produce, but are not
permitted to carry from them directly to our
own country their principal manufactures
or produce. The people to whom we are
thus permitted to fell, want the principal inducement for dealing with us, and the great
fpring of commerce, which is mutual exchange, is wanting between us,

As the Britifh legiflature has thought it
reafonable to extend, in a very confiderable
degree, our exportation to their colonies, and ·
has doubtlefs intended that this favour fhould
be ufeful to Ireland, it is hoped that thofe
reftraints on the importation from thence,
which muft render that favour of little effect, will be no longer continued.

From

From thofe confiderations it is evident that many ftrong reafons refpecting Ireland are now to be found againft the continuance of thofe reftrictive laws of 1663 and 1670, that did not exift at the time of making them.

The prohibition of 1699 was immediately and univerfally felt in this country; but in the courfe of human events various and powerful reafons have arifen againft the continuance of that ftatute, which did not exift, and could not have been forefeen when it was enacted.

At the reftoration the inhabitants of Ireland confifted of three different nations, Englifh, Scotch and Irifh, divided by political and religious princip'es, exafperated against each other by former animofities, and by prefent contefts for property. When the fettlement of the country was compleated, the people became induftrious, manufactures greatly increafed, and the kingdom began to flourifh. The prohibition of exporting cattle to England, and, perhaps, that

of

of importing directly from America the materials of other manufactures, obliged the
Irish to increafe, and to manufacture their
own material. They made fo great a progrefs in both, from 1672 to 1687, that in
the latter year the exports of the woollen
manufacture alone amounted in value to
70,521l. 14s. od.

But the religious and civil animofities continued. The papifts objected to the fettlement of property made after the reftoration *,
wifhed to reverfe the outlawries and to ref-
cind the laws on which that fettlement was
founded, hoped to eftablifh their own as the
national religion, to get the power of the
kingdom into their own hands, and to effect
all thofe purpofes by a king of their own religion. They endeavoured to attain all thofe
objects by laws † paffed at a meeting, which
they called a parliament, held under this
prince

* Carte, 2 Vol. 425 to 428, 465.
† Archb. Bifhop King's State, 209. James the 2d in his
fpeech from the throne in Ireland, recommended the repeal
of the act of fettlement.

prince after his abdication ; and by their conduct at this period, as well as in the year
1642 *, fhewed difpofitions unfavourable to
the fubordination of Ireland to the crown of
England. They could not be fuppofed to be
well affected to that great Prince who de-
feated all their purpofes.

At the time of the revolution the numbers of our people were again very much reduced ; but a great majority of the remaining inhabitants confifted of papifts. Thofe,
notwithftanding their difappointment at
that æra, were thought to entertain expectations of the refloration of their popifh king,
and defigns unfavorable to the eftablifhed
conftitution in church and ftate. It is not
to the prefent purpofe to inquire how long
this

* Their demands in 1642 were the reftitution of all the
plantation lands to the old inhabitants, repeal of Poyning's
act, &c. Macaulay's Hift. 3 Vol. 222. In the meeting,
called a parliament, held by James in Ireland, they repealed
the acts of fettlement and explanation, paffed a law that
the parliament of England cannot bind Ireland, and againft
writs of error and appeals to England.

this difpofition prevailed. It cannot be
doubted but that this was the opinion con-
ceived of their views and principles at the
time of paffing this law of the year 1699.

England could not then confider a country under fuch unfortunate circumftances as
any great additional ftrength to it. Foreign
proteftants were invited to fettle in it, and
the emigration of papifts in great numbers
to other countries was allowed, if not encouraged. Though at this period a regard
to liberty as well as to œconomy, occafioned
the difbanding of all the army in England,
except 7000, it was thought neceffary for
the fecurity of Ireland that an army of
12,000 men fhould be kept there; and for
many years afterwards it was not allowed
that this army fhould be recruited in this
kingdom. This diftinction of parties in Ireland was in thofe times the main fpring in
every movement relative to that kingdom,
and affected not only political but commercial regulations. The reafon affigned by
the Englifh ftatute, allowing the exportation
of

of Irifh linen cloth to the plantations, is, after reciting the reftrictive law of 1663*,
"*yet* forafmuch as the proteftant intereft of
" Ireland ought to be fupported, by giving
" the utmoft encouragement to the linen
" manufactures of that kingdom, in tender
" regard to her majefty's good proteftant
" fubjects of her faid kingdom, be it enact-
" ed," &c.

The papifts, then difabled from acquiring
permanent property in lands, had not the
fame intereft with proteftants in the defence of their country and in the profperity
of the Britifh empire. But thofe feeds of
difunion and diffidence no longer remain.
No man looks now for the return of the ex-
iled family, any more than for that of Per-
ken Warbec; and the repeal of magna
charta is as much expected as of the act of
fettlement. The papifts, indulged with the
exercife of their religious worfhip, and now
at liberty to acquire permanent property

in

* 3d and 4th Anne, ch. 8.

in lands, are intereſted as well as proteſtants
in the fecurity and profperity of this country; and fenfible of the benign influence
of our fovereign, and of the protection and
happinefs which they enjoy under his reign,
feem to be as well affected to the king and
to the conſtitution of the ſtate as any other
clafs of fubjects, and at this moſt dangerous
crifis have contributed their money to raife
men for his majeſty's fervice, and declared
their readinefs, had the laws permitted, to
have taken arms for the defence of their
country. They owe much to the favour
and protection of the crown, and to the
liberal and benevolent fpirit of the Britiſh
legiflature which led the way to their relief,
and they are peculiarly interefted to cultivate the good opinion of their fovereign,
and of their fellow-fubjects in Great Britain.

The numbers of our people, fince the
year 1698, are more than doubled; but in
point of real ftrength to the Britiſh empire
are increafed in a proportion of above eight

to one. In the year 1698, the numbers of
our people did not much, if at all, exceed
one million. Of thefe 500,000 are thought
to be a liberal allowance for proteftants of
all denominations. It is now fuppofed
that there are not lefs in this kingdom than
2,500,000 inhabitants, loyal and affectionate
fubjects to his majefty, and well-affected to
the conftitution and happinefs of their
country.

A political and commercial conftitution, if
it could have been confidered as wifely framed
for the years 1663, 1670 and 1698, ought
to be reconfidered in the year 1779; what
mighthave been good and neceffary policy in
the government of one million of men difu-
nited among themfelves, and a majority of
them not to be relied upon in fupport of
their king and of the laws and conftitution
of their country, is bad policy in the
government of two millions and a half of
men now united among themfelves, and all
interefted in the fupport of the crown, the
laws, and the conftitution.

What

What might have been fufficient employment, and the means of acquiring a compe-
tent fubfiftence for one million of people,
when a man by working two days in the
week might have earned a fufficient fupport
for him and his family, will never anfwer
for two millions and a half of people *,
when the hard labour of fix days in the
week can fcarcely fupply a fcanty fubfiftence.   Nor can the refources which enabled us in the laft century to remit 200,000l.
yearly to England †, fupport remittances to
the amount of more than fix times that
fum.

Let the reafons for this reftrictive fyftem
at the time of its formation be examined,
and let us judge impartially, whether any
one of the purpofes then intended has been
anfwered.   The reafons refpecting America,
were to confine the Plantation-trade to England, and to make that country a ftore-
houfe of all commodities for its colonies.
But

* Sir W. Petty's Survey.
† Ib. 117.

But the commercial jealoufy that has prevailed among the different ftates of Europe,
has made it difficult for any nation to keep
great markets to herfelf in exclufion of the
reft of the world.   It was not forefeen at
thofe periods that the colonies, whilft they
all continued dependent, fhould have traded
with foreign nations, notwithftanding the
utmoft efforts of Great Britain to prevent
it.   It was not forefeen that thofe colonies
would have refufed to have taken any commodities whatever from their parent country, that they fhould afterwards have fepa-
rated themfelves from her empire, declared
themfelves independent, refifted her fleets
and armies, obtained the moft powerful
alliances, and occafioned the moft dangerous and deftructive war in which Great Britain was ever engaged.   Nor could it have
been forefeen that Ireland, excluded from almoft all direct intercoufe with them, fhould
have been nearly undone by the conteft.
The reafons then refpecting America no
longer exift, and whatever may be the event
of the conflict, will never exift to the extent
expected

expected when this fyftem of reftraints and penalties was adopted.

The reafons relating to Ireland have failed alfo. The circumftances of this country relative to the woollen manufacture are totally changed fince the year 1699. The lords and commons of England appear to have founded the law of that year on the proportion which they fuppofed that the charge of the woollen manufacture in England then bore to the charge of that manufacture in Ireland. In the reprefentation from the commiffioners of trade, laid before both houfes †, they think it a reafonable conjecture to take the difference between both wool and labour in the two countries to be one third; and eftimating on that fuppofition, they find that 43½ per cent, may be laid on broad cloth exported out of Ireland, more than on the like cloth exported out of England, to bring them both

to

† Order 14th March 1698, Lords Journ. v. 16.   Eng. Com. Journs. 18th Jan. 1698, 12 v. 440.

to an equality. This muſt have been an alarming reprefentation to England.

But if thoſe calculations were juſt at the time, which is very doubtful, the fuppofed faĉts on which they were founded do certainly no longer exiſt. Wool is now generally at a higher price in Ireland than in England, and the trifling difference in the price of labour is more than over-balanced by this and the other circumſtances in favour of England, which have been before ſtated; and that thoſe faĉts fuppofed in 1698, and the inferences drawn from them, have no foundation in the prefent ſtate of this country is plain from the experience of every day, which ſhews that inſtead of our underfelling the Engliſh, they underfell us in our own markets.

Befides our excluſion from foreign markets, England had two objeĉts in the difcouragement of our woollen trade.

It was intended that Ireland ſhould fend her wool to England, and take from ʰ at

ʰ   ᵗry

country her woollen manufactures *. It has been already shewn that the first object has not been attained; the second has been carried so far as, for the future, to defeat its own purpose. Whilst our own manufacturers were starving for want of employment, and our wool sold for less than one half of its usual price, we have imported from England in the years 1777 and 1778 woollen goods to the enormous amount of 715,740l 13s od as valued at our custom-house, and of the manufactures of linen, cotton and silk mixed, to the amount of 98,086l 1s 11d, making in the whole in

P   those

---

* The commissioners of trade, in their representation dated the 11th November 1697, relating to the trade between England and Ireland, advise a duty to be laid upon the importation of oil, upon teasles, whether imported or *growing* there, and upon *all the utensils* employed in the making any woollen manufactures, on the utensils of worsted-combers, and particularly a duty by the yard upon all cloth and woollen stuffs, except frizes, before they are taken off the loom. Eng. Com. Journ. v. 428.

thofe two years of diftrefs 813,826l 14s 11d†. Between 20 and 30,000 of our manufacturers in thofe branches were in thofe two years fupported by public charity. From this fact it is hoped that every reafonable man will allow the neceffity of our ufing our own manufactures. Agreements among our people for this purpofe are not, as it has been fuppofed, a new idea in this country. It was never fo univerfal as at prefent, but has been frequently reforted' to in times of diftrefs. In the feffions of 1703, 1705 and 1707‡, the houfe of commons refolved unanimoufly, that it would greatly conduce to the relief of the poor and the good of the kingdom, that the inhabitants thereof fhould ufe none other but the manufactures of this kingdom in their apparel and the furniture of their houfes; and in the laft of thofe feffions the members engaged their honours

† See in the appendix an account of thofe articles imported from England into Ireland, for ten years, commencing in 1769, and ending in 1778.

‡ Com. Journ. 3 vol. 348, 548.

honours to each other, that they would conform to the faid refolution. The not importing goods from England is one of the remedies recommended by the council of ` trade in 1676 for alleviating fome diftrefs that was felt at that time *; and fir William Temple, a zealous friend to the trade and manufactures of England, recommends to lord Effex, then lord lieutenant, " to intro- " duce as far as can be, a vein of parfimony " throughout the country, in all things that " are not perfectly the native growths and " manufactures .§"

The people of England can not reafona- ably object to a conduct of which they have given a memorable example ‡. In 1697 the Englifh houfe of lords prefented an addrefs to king William to difcourage the ufe and wearing of all forts of furniture and cloths, not of the growth or manufac-

ture

---

* Sir W. Petty's Political Survey, 125.
§ Sir W. Temple, 3 v. 11.
‡ Lords Journ. 16th Feb. 1697.

ture of that kingdom, and befeech him by his royal example effectually to encourage the ufe and wearing of all forts of furniture and wearing cloths that are the growth of that kingdom, or manufactured there; and king William affures them that he would give the example to his fubjects †, and would endeavour to make it effectually followed. The reafon affigned by the lords for this addrefs was, that the trade of the nation had fuffered by the late long and expenfive war. But it does not appear that there was any preffing neceffity at the time, or that their manufacturers were ftarving for want of employment.

Common fenfe muft difcover to every man that, where foreign trade is reftrained, difcouraged, or prevented in any country, and where that country has the materials of manufactures, a fruitful foil, and numerous inhabitants, the home-trade is its beft refource. If this is thought, by men of great knowledge, to be the moft valuable of all trades,

Lords Journ. 19th Feb. 1697.

trades §, becaufe it makes the fpeedieft and the fureft returns, and becaufe it increafes at the fame time two capitals in the fame country, there is no nation on the globe, whofe wealth, population, ftrength and happinefs would be promoted by fuch a trade in a greater degree than ours *.

Two other reafons were affigned for this prohibition,—that the Irifh had fhewn themfelves unwilling to promote the linen manufacture †; and that there were great quantities of wool in Ireland. But they have fince cultivated the linen trade with great fuccefs, and great numbers of their people

§ See Dr. Smith's Wealth of Nations.

* The confumption of our own people is the beft and greateft market for the product and manufactures of our own country. Foreign trade is but a part of the benefit arifing from the woollen manufacture, and the leaft part ; it is a fmall article in refpect to the benefit arifing to the community; and Dr. Smith affirms that all the foreign markets of England cannot be equal to one-twentieth part of her own. Dr. Smith's memoirs of wool, 2 vol. 113, 529, 530 and 556, from the Britifh merchant and Dr. Davenant.

† Addrefs of Eng. Commons, ante.

people are employed in it. Of late years, by the
operation of the land-carriage bounty agriculture has increafed in a degree never before
known in this country; extenfive tracts of
lands, formerly fheep-pafture, are now under tillage, and much greater rents are
given for that purpofe than can be paid by
ftocking with fheep; the quantity of wool
is greatly diminifhed from what it was in
the year 1699, fuppofing it to have been
then equal to the quantity in 1687*; it has
been for feveral years leffening, and is not
likely to be increafed.   In thofe two important circumftances the grounds of the
apprehenfions of England have ceafed, and
the ftate of Ireland has been materially altered fince the year 1699.

Another reafon refpecting England and
foreign ftates, particularly France, has
failed.   England was in 1698, in poffeffion
of the woollen trade in moft of the foreign
markets, and expected ftill to continue to
                                        fupply

---

* King's Stat. 160, 161.

fupply them, as appears by the preamble of her ftatute paffed in that year.

She at that time expected to keep this manufacture to herfelf. The people of Leeds, Hallifax and Newberry † petition the houfe of commons, " that by fome means " the woollen manufacture may be prevent- " ed from being fet up in foreign countries;" and the commons in their addrefs, mention the keeping it as much as poffible *entire* to themfelves. But experience has proved the vanity of thofe expectations; feveral other countries cultivate this trade with fuccefs. France now underfells her. England has loft fome of thofe markets, and it is thought probable that Ireland, if admitted to them, might have preferved and may now recover the trade that England has loft.

A perfeverance in this reftrictive policy will be ruinous to the trade of Great Britain. Whatever may be the ftate of America, great numbers of the inhabitants of Ireland, if the circumftances of this country fhall continue to be the fame as at prefent in refpect of

† Eng. Com. Journ. 12 v. 514, 523, 528.

of trade, will emigrate there; this will give
ſtrength to that part of the empire on which
Great Britain can leaſt, and take it from that
part on which at preſent ſhe may moſt ſecure-
ly depend. But this is not all the miſchief;
thoſe emigrants will be moſtly manufacturers, and will transfer to America the woollen and linen manufactures, to the great
prejudice of thoſe trades in England, Scotland and Ireland; and then one of the
means uſed to keep the colonies dependent,
by introducing this country into a ſyſtem of
colonization, will be the occaſion of leſſen-
ing, if not diſſolving, the connection between them and their parent ſtate.

Great Britain, weakened in her extremities,
ſhould fortify the heart of her empire;
Great Britain, with powerful foreign enemies united in laſting bonds againſt her,
and with ſcarcely any foreign alliance to
ſuſtain her, ſhould exert every poſſible effort
to ſtrengthen herſelf at home. The numbers of people in Ireland have more than
doubled in fourſcore years. How much more
rapid would be the increaſe if the growth of
the

the human race was cherifhed by finding fufficient employment and food for this prolific
nation! it would probably double again in
half a century.   What a vaft acceffion of
ftrength fuch numbers of brave and active
men, living almoft within the found of a
trumpet, muft bring to Great Britain, now
faid to be decreafing confiderably in population! a greater certainly than double thofe
numbers difperfed in diftant parts of the
globe, the expence of defending and go-
verning of which muft at all times be great.
Sir W. Temple * in 1673 takes notice of the
circumftances prejudicial to the trade and
riches of Ireland, which had hitherto, he
fays, made it of more lofs than value to
England. They have already been mentioned. The courfe of time has removed fome
of them, and the wifdom and philantrophy
of Britain may remove the reft.   " Without
" thefe circumftances, (fays that honeft and
" able ftatefman,) the native fertility of the
" foils and feas in fo many rich commodities,
                              " improved

" improved by multitudes of people and in-
" duſtry, with the advantage of ſo many ex-
" cellent havens, and a ſituation ſo commo-
" dious for all ſorts of foreign trade, muſt
" needs have rendered this kingdom one of
" the richeſt in Europe, and made a mighty
" increaſe both of ſtrength and revenue to
" the crown of England *."

During this century Ireland has been
without exaggeration, a mine of wealth to
England, far beyond what any calculation
has yet made it.   When poor and thinly inhabited ſhe was an expence and a burden to
England; when ſhe had acquired ſome proportion of riches and grew more numerous,
ſhe was one of the principal ſources of her
wealth. When ſhe becomes poor again, thoſe
advantages are greatly diminiſhed.   The exports from Great Britain to Ireland in 1778 †
were leſs, that the medium value of the four
preceding

* See Sir John Davis's Diſcourſes, p. 5, 6, 194.

† Summary of imports and exports to and from Ireland,
laid before the Britiſh houſe of commons in 1779.

preceding years in a fum of 634,444l. 3s. od;
and in the year 1779 Great Britain is obliged,
partly at her own expence, to defend this
country, and for that purpofe has generoufly
beftowed out of her own exchequer a large
fum of money.   Thofe facts demonftrate
that the poverty of Ireland ever has been a
drain, and her riches an influx of wealth to
England, to which the greater part of it
will ever flow, and it imports not to that
country through what channel: but the
fource muft be cleared from obftructions, or
the ftream cannot continue to flow.

Such a liberal fyftem would increafe the
wealth of this kingdom by means that would
ftrengthen the hands of government, and
promote the happinefs of the people.   Ireland would be then able to contribute large-
ly to the fupport of the Britifh empire, not
only from the increafe of her wealth, but
from the more equal diftribution of it into
a greater number of hands among the various
orders of the community.   The prefent inability of Ireland arifes principally from this
                                        circumftance,

circumftance, that her lower and middle claffes have little or no property, and are not
able, to any confiderable amount, either to
pay taxes, or to confume thofe commodities
that are the ufual fubjects of them; and this
has been the confequence of the laws which
prevent trade and difcourage manufactures.
The fame quantity of property diftributed
through the different claffes of the people
would fupply refources much fuperior to
thofe which can be found in the prefent
ftate of Ireland *. The increafe of people
there under its prefent reftraints makes but
a fmall addition to the refources of the ftate
in refpect of taxes†. In 1685 the amount

* Thofe ftates are leaft able to pay great charge for public difburfements, whofe wealth refteth chiefly in the hands
of the nobility and gentry. Bac. 1 Vol. p. 10. Smith's
Wealth of Nations, 2 Vol. p. 22.

† A very judicious friend of mine has, with great pains
and attention, made a calculation of the numbers of people
in Ireland in the year 1774, and he makes the numbers of
people to amount to 2,325,041, but fuppofes his calculation to be under the real number. I have therefore followed
the calculation commonly received, which makes their
number

of the inland excife in Ireland was 75,169l.
In 1762 it increafed only to 92,842l. Thofe
years are taken as periods of a confiderable
degree of profperity in Ireland. The people
had increafed from 1685 to 1762 in a proportion of nearly 7 to 4*, which appears
from this circumftance, that in 1685 hearth
money amounted to 32,659l. and in 1762 to
56,611l. At the former period the law made
to reftrain and difcourage the principal trade
and manufacture of Ireland had not been
made. There were then vaft numbers of
fheep in Ireland, and the woollen manufacture was probably in a flourifhing ftate. At
the former of thofe periods the lower claffes
of the people were able to confume excifable

commo-

number amount to 2,500,000. He computes, as has been
before mentioned, the perfons who refide in houfes of
one hearth, to be 1,877,220. Thofe find it very difficult
to pay hearth-money, and are thought to be unable to pay
any other taxes. If this is fo, according to this calculation,
there are but 447,821 people in Ireland able to pay taxes.

* Ireland was much more numerous in 1685 than at any
time, after the revolution, during that century, there having been a great wafte of people in the rebellion at that
æra.

commodities. In the latter they lived for the moſt part on the immediate produce of the foil. The numbers of people in a ſtate, like thoſe of a private family, if the individuals have the means of acquiring, add to the wealth, and if they have not thoſe means, to the poverty of the community. Population is not always a proof of the proſperity of a nation; the people may be very numerous, and very poor and wretched. A temperate climate, fruitful foil, bays and rivers well ſtocked with fiſh, the habits of life among the lower claſſes, and a long peace, are ſufficient to increaſe the numbers of people; theſe are the true wealth of every ſtate that has wiſdom to encourage the induſtry of its inhabitants, and a country which ſupplies in abundance the materials for that induſtry. If the ſtate, or the family ſhould diſcourage induſtry, and not allow one of the family to work, becauſe another is of the ſame trade, the conſequences to the great or the little community, muſt be equally fatal.

Is

Is there not bufinefs enough in this great world for the people of two adjoining iflands without depreffing the inhabitants of one of them? let the magnanimity and philanthrophy of Great Britain addrefs her poor fifter kingdom in the fame language which the good-natured uncle Toby ufes to the fly, in fetting it at liberty—" poor fly, there's room enough for thee and me !"

I have the honour to be,

My Lord, &c.

THE

THE

COMMERCIAL RESTRAINTS

OF

IRELAND

CONSIDERED.

NINTH LETTER.

Q

THE

COMMERCIAL RESTRAINTS

OF

IRELAND

CONSIDERED.

NINTH LETTER.

My Lord,

Dublin, 10th Sept. 1779.

BESIDES thofe already mentioned, various other commercial reftraints and prohibi-
tions give the Britifh trader and manufacturer many great and important advantages
over the Irifh. Whilft our markets are at
all times open to all their productions and
manufactures, with inconfiderable duties on
the import, their markets are open or fhut
againft us as fuits their conveniency. On
feveral articles of the firft importance, and
on almoft all our own manufactures, im-

Q 2   ported

ported into Great Britain, duties are imposed equal to a prohibition. In the instance of woollen-goods, their's in our ports pay but a small duty, our's in their ports are loaded with duties *, which amount to a prohibition † ; their's on the exportation are subject to no duty ; our's, if permitted to be exported, would, as the law now stands, be subject to a duty ‡ over and above that payable for alnage and for the alnager's fee. If the act of 1699 was repealed, the English would still have many great advantages over us in the woollen trade.

In our staple manufacture, the bounties given on the exportation of white and brown

Irish

* 12th Ch. II. ch. 4. Eng.

† Yet in favour of Great Britain, old and new drapery imported into Ireland from other countries are subject to duties equal to a prohibition. Ir. act 14th and 15th Ch. II. ch. 8.

‡ On every piece of old drapery exported, containing 36 yards, and so for a greater or lesser quantity 3s. 4d. and of new drapery 9d. for the subsidy of alnage and alnager's fee. See 17th and 18th Ch. II. ch. 15. Ir. But the English have taken off these and all other duties from their manufactures made or mixed with wool. Eng. act 11 and 12 W. III. ch. 20.

Irifh linen from Great-Britain would ftill continue that trade in the hands of the Britifh merchant. On all coloured linens a duty* equal to a prohibition is impofed on the importation into Great-Britain; but their's imported to us are fubject + to ten per cent, and under that duty they have imported confiderably. This inequality of duty and the bounty given by the Britifh act of the tenth of Geo. the 3d on the exportation of their chequered and ftriped linens from Great-Britain, fecures to them the continuance of the great fuperiority which they have acquired over us in thofe very valuable branches of this trade. In many other articles they have given themfelves great advantages. Beer they export to us in fuch quantities as almoft to ruin our brewery; but they prevent our exportation to them by duties, laid on the import there, equal to a prohibition. Of malt they make large exports to us, to the prejudice of our agriculture, but have abfolutely

---

* Thirty per cent. by the Britifh acts of 9 and 12 Anne, ch. 39, and 12 Anne, ch. 9.

† This tax is ad valorem, and the linen not valued.

abfolutely prohibited our exportation of that
commodity to them.   Some manufactures
they retain folely to themfelves, which we
are prohibited from exporting, and cannot
import from any country but Great Britain,
as glafs of all kinds.   Hops they do not allow us to import from any other place, and
in a facetious ftyle of interdiction pronounce
fuch importation to be a common nuifance *.
They go further, and by laying a duty on
the export, and denying the draw-back, ob-
lige the Irifh confumer to pay a tax appro-
priated, it is faid, to the payment of a Britifh debt.   I fhall make no political, but the
fubject requires a commercial obfervation—
it is this—the man who keeps a market folely to himfelf in exclufion of all others, whether he appears as buyer † or feller,   fixes
his own price, and becomes the arbiter of the
profit and lofs of every cuftomer,

The

---

* Brit. Act, 9 Ann. ch. 12.

† Hence it is that the price of wool in England is faid
to be 50 per cent. below the market price of Europe.
Smith's Memoirs of wool.

The various manufactures * made or mixed with cotton, are subject by several British acts to duties on the importation, amounting to 25 per cent.

By another act, penalties † are impofed on wearing any of thofe manufactures in Great-Britain, unlefs made in that country. Thofe laws have effectually excluded the Irifh manufactures in all thofe branches from the British markets, and it has been already fhewn, that they cannot be fent to the American. From Great Britain into Ireland all thofe articles are imported in immenfe quantities, being fubject here to duties amounting to ten per cent. only.

But it would be tedious to defcend into a further detail, and difgufting to write a book of rates inftead of a letter ‡.

---

* 12 Ch. II. ch. 5. 3 and 4 Ann. ch. 4. 4 and 5 W. and M. ch. 5.

† 7 G. 1. ch. 7.

‡ When the commercial reftraints of Ireland are the fubject, a fource of occafional and ruinous reftrictions ought not

Their fuperior capitals and expertnefs, give them decifive advantages in every fpecies of trade and manufacture. By the extenfion of the commerce of Ireland, Great Britain would acquire new and important advantages, not only by the wealth it would bring to that country, and the encreafe of ftrength to the empire, but by opening to the Britifh merchant new fources of trade from Ireland.

It is time to draw to a conclufion. I have reviewed my letters to your lordfhip for the purpofe of avoiding every poffible occafion of offence; I flatter myfelf every reader will difcern that they have been written with upright and friendly intentions, not to excite jealoufies but to remove prejudices, to moderate and conciliate, and that they are intended as an appeal, not to the paffions of the multitude, but to the wifdom, juftice and generofity of Britain. Shakefpeare could

place

not to be paffed over. Since the year 1740, there have been 24 embargoes in Ireland, one of which lafted three years.

place a tongue in every wound of Cæſar,
but Antony meant to inflame; and the only
purpofe of thofe letters is to perfuade. I
have therefore not even removed the mantle
except where neceffity required it.

In extraordinary cafes where the facts are
ſtronger than the voice of the pleader, it is
not unufual to allow the client to fpeak for
himfelf. Will you, my lord, one of the lead-
ing advocates for Ireland, allow her to addreſs
her elder fifter, and to ſtate her own cafe;
not in the ſtrains of paffion or refentment,
nor in the tone of remonſtrance, but with
a modeſt enumeration of unexaggerated facts
in pathetic fimplicity; fhe will tell her, with
a countenance full of affection and tender-
nefs, " I have received from you invalua-
" ble gifts, the law of * common right, your
" great charter, and the fundamentals of your
" conftitution. The temple of liberty in
" your country, has been frequently fortifi-
" ed, improved and embellifhed ; mine erect-
" ed

* The common law of England.

" ed many centuries fince the perfect mo-
" del of your own ; you will not fuffer me
" to ftrengthen, fecure, or repair; firm and
" well cemented as it is, it muft moulder un-
" der the hand of Time for want of that at-
" tention, which is due to the venerable
" fabrick *. We are connected by the ftrong-
" eft ties of natural affection, common fecu-
" rity, and a long interchange of the kindeft
" offices on both fides. But for more than a
" century you have, in fome inftances, mif-
" taken our mutual intereft. I fent you my
" herds and my flocks, filled your people
" with abundance, and gave them leifure
" to attend to more profitable purfuits, than
" the humble employment of fhepherds and
" of herds-men. But you rejected my pro-
" duce †, and reprobated this intercourfe in
" terms the moft opprobrious. I fubmitted;
" the temporary lofs was mine, but the per-
" petual

---

* Heads of bills for paffing into a law the habeas corpus
act, and that for making the tenure of judges during good
behaviour, have repeatedly paffed the Irifh houfe of commons, but were not returned.

† The Eng. act of Ch. II. ch.   calls the importation
of cattle from Ireland, a common nufance.

" petual prejudice your own. I incited my
" children to induſtry, and gave them my
" principal materials to manufacture. Their
" honeſt labours were attended with mode-
" rate ſuccefs, but fufficient to awaken the
" commercial jealoufy of fome of your fons;
" indulging their groundlefs apprehenſions,
" you defired my materials and difcouraged
" the induſtry of my people. I complied
" with your wiſhes, and gave to your chil-
" dren the bread of my own; but the ene-
" mies of our race were the gainers; they
" applied themfelves with tenfold encreafe
" to thofe purfuits which were reſtrained in
" my people, who would have added to the
" wealth and ſtrength of your empire what
" by this fatal error you transfered to fo-
" reign nations. You held out another ob-
" ject to me with promifes of the utmoſt
" encouragement. I wanted the means, but
" I obtained them from other countries, and
" have long cultivated, at great expence and
" with the moſt unremitted efforts, that
" fpecies of induſtry which you recommend-
" ed. You foon united with another great
" family,

" family, engaged in the fame purfuit,
" which you were alfo obliged to encourage
" among them, and afterwards embarked in
" it yourfelf, and became my rival in that
" which you had deftined for my principal
" fupport. This fupport is now become
" inadequate to the encreafed number of
" my offspring, many of whom want the
" means of fubfiftence. My ports are ever
" hofpitably open for your reception, and
" fhut, whenever your intereft requires it,
" againft all others; but your's are in many
" inftances barred againft me, with your
" dominions in Afia, Africa and America;
" my fons were long deprived of all benefi-
" cial intercourfe, and yet to thofe colonies
" I tranfported my treafures for the payment
" of your armies, and in a war waged
" for their defence, one hundred thoufand
" of my fons fought by your fide *. Con-
" queft attended our arms. You gained a
" great increafe of empire and of commerce;
" and

* This number of Irifhmen was computed to have ferved in the fleets and armies of Great Britain during the laft
war.

" and my people a further extenfion of re-
" ftraints and prohibitions†. In thofe ef-
" forts I have exhaufted my ftrength, mort-
" gaged my territories, and am now finking
" under the preffure of enormous debts con-
" tracted from my zealous attachment to
" your interefts, to the extenfion of your .
" empire and the encreafe of your glory.
" By the prefent unhappy war for the reco-
" very of thofe colonies, from which they
" were long excluded, my children are re-
" duced to the loweft ebb of poverty and
" diftrefs. It is true, you have lately with
" the kindeft intentions, allowed me an ex-
" tenfive liberty of felling to the inhabitants
" of thofe parts of your empire, but they
" have no inducement to buy, becaufe I can-
" not take their produce in return. Your
" liberality has opened a new fountain, but
" your

† The Furs of Canada, the Indigo of Florida, the
fugars of Dominica, St. Vincent's and the Grenades, with
every other valuable production of thofe acquifitions, Ireland was prohibited to receive but through another channel. Her poverty fcarcely gathered a crum from the fump-
tuous table of her fifter.

" your caution will not fuffer me to draw
" from it. The ftream of commerce, intend-
" ed to refrefh the exhaufted ftrength of my
" children, flies untafted from their parched
" lips.

" The common parent of all has been e-
" qually beneficent to us both. We both
" poffefs in great abundance the means
" of induftry and of happinefs. My fields
" are not lefs fertile, nor my harbours lefs
" numerous than your's. My fons are not
" lefs renowned than your own for valour,
" juftice and generofity. Many of them
" are your defcendants, and have fome of
" your beft blood in their veins. But the
" narrow policy of man has counteracted
" the inftincts and the bounties of nature.
" In the midft of thofe fertile fields, fome of
" my children perifh before my eyes for want
" of food, and others fly for refuge to hof-
" tile nations.

" Suffer

" Suffer no longer, refpected fifter, the
" narrow jealoufy of commerce to miflead
" the wifdom and to impair the ftrength of
" the ftate. Encreafe my refources, they
" fhall be your's, my riches and ftrength, my
" poverty and weaknefs will become your
" own. What a triumph to our enemies,
" and what an affliction to me, in the pre-
" fent diftracted circumftances of the em-
" pire, to fee my people reduced, by the
" neceffity of avoiding famine, to the refo-
" lution of traficking almoft folely with
" themfelves! great and powerful enemies
" are combined againft you, many of your
" diftant connections have deferted you,
" encreafe your ftrength at home, open
" and extend the numerous refources of my
" country, of which you have not hitherto
" availed yourfelf or allowed me the benefit.
" Our encreafed force and the full exertions
" of our ftrength will be the moft effectual
" means of refifting the combination formed
" againft you by foreign enemies and diftant
                              " fubjects,

" fubjects, and of giving new luftre to our
" crowns, and happinefs and contentment to
" our people."

T H E   E N D.

Since thefe papers were fent to the prefs, the Commons of Ireland have, in their ad-drefs to his majefty, refolved unanimoufly, " that it is not by temporary expediènts, " but by a free trade alone that this nation " is now to be faved from impending ruin". And the lords have in their addrefs unani-moufly entered into a refolution of the famę import.